The author writes under a pen name. She has dyslexia but refuses to let it hold her back, seeing it as a challenge to be met. She was born and raised in rural Ireland and has a great love of the environment. Her other great loves include family, friends and music.

For my family and friends

Nina Ryan

ATLANTIS RISE

AUSTIN MACAULEY PUBLISHERS™

LONDON ∗ CAMBRIDGE ∗ NEW YORK ∗ SHARJAH

A CIP catalogue record for this title is available from the British Library.

ISBN 9781398445949 (Paperback)
ISBN 9781398445956 (ePub e-book)

www.austinmacauley.com

First Published 2022
Austin Macauley Publishers Ltd®
1 Canada Square
Canary Wharf
London
E14 5AA

Many thanks to the teams at Austin Macauley Publishers Ltd.

Atlantis rise

Long before the last ice age, there was a golden era where all people from all walks of life lived together and prospered. Atlantis was at the height of its power and the centre of the world. But one day came to pass that would change history and the lives of everyone. All ages come to an end and so too this age passed, greed corrupted man's heart and war broke out. They fought for land, resources, knowledge, ideas and different beliefs they held. The King of Atlantis, lost in his greed, used the very power at the heart of Atlantis to cast a spell that would bind all peoples to him. However, his greed was so great that the spell went awry and humans lost the ability to sense magic. The gods, seeing the rising of man and his follies, struck Atlantis down and waves and fire fell upon the great city. The King fell with Atlantis.

The Descendants of Hades, as they were called, were said to have fiendish hearts and their magic was a dark and terrible thing. The leader of the Descendants hoped to use the curse to rule the humans now that they were weakened. To take the power of the kings and rule Atlantis.

But the Atlantis High Council were born forbidding another king. A terrible war followed where the Descendants were destroyed and the power of Atlantis was lost. The high council searched the world for a cure but to no avail. The Atlantis became solely ruled by the high council and the dead king became the last king of Atlantis.

The humans fled Atlantis that they had shared with the other peoples of the Earth. They soon forgot their magic and the Atlantis high counsel ruled to let the humans lead their own lives as no one could help them.

Human history remembers Atlantis as a legend, a lesson, and Atlantis became a shade to its former self.

Part One
Atlantis Fire

Chapter 1
Chameleon

The steel ship shuddered violently and lost altitude in a sudden drop, Ali fell over but was faring better than Jenks, who was being sat on by a dog called Rex. Yuki struggled to pull out Jenks from under Rex and told him that he had been the runt of the litter.

'So you keep telling us,' said Jenks dryly and tried to brush off the fur that his coat had collected. Ali could remember the day that Yuki and she had picked up Rex and it was true that he had been the runt of the litter but for Yuki, it was love at first sight. Nearly everyone in her family had an affinity with one animal or another so it was no surprise when Yuki applied for a ship sense guide.

'What was that Reece?' shouted Captain Philip. Rolling out of one of the bunk beds in the back of the plane.

'Fuel is running low, captain,' called back Reece. 'I think there is some damage to the fuel tank, a slow leak by the system only picking it up now.'

'Right ladies and gentlemen, we are not making it home tonight. Nav, you better find a base for tonight,' announced Captain Philip, shrugging on a long brown coat.

Ali worked on her charts on the centre table, 'If we turn north now, we should make it to Athens with the fuel that is left, Rome is our second option but from a report earlier today there are antihuman riots, meaning the base will be full.' The capital cities, human and non-human, always held the largest bases as it was easier to hide them.

'Athens, it is then,' called Reece, taking the charts from Ali, then the ship banked right. 'We are going to have to run a lower power but we will make it there with no problem.' The ship lights dim, casting angular shadows and the pale grey interior creating darkness to the eye.

'I have never been to Greece before. I wonder what it will be like?' Pondered Yuki as she stood to feed Rex, who ate more than everyone on the ship put together.

'It will be dark that's what it will be like. We are only staying the night and leaving before first light and no one is allowed to leave the base,' commanded Philip as he marched through the cabin.

Yuki placed a huge wooden bowl of food on the floor for Rex and smiled as she rose. 'That's okay, I can see in the dark.' Yuki blinked, her pupils becoming cat-like slits.

'Freaks me out every time,' shuddered Jenks.

'Reece, you better keep this ship level, I have to call Athens to let them know we are coming and I don't want to be falling all over the place,' said Captain Philip then he left them climbing the metal spiral staircase to the mezzanine bridge. There he picked up the messenger, a small translucent orb from the centre of the map table. Captain Philip placed his hand on the orb, pouring magic into the glass bobble. It glowed green with the captain's earth magic. Suddenly, the other half of the orb turned blue, someone had responded they must have water magic judging by the colour, thought Ali.

*

'It's beautiful,' admired Yuki but all Ali could see was lights in the dark and Jenks couldn't see much either.

'We are coming up on the base now if everyone would like to take their seats and remain seated till we have landed and the seat belt light is turned off,' Reece instructed in his best formal voice.

'Reece, we don't have that light,' called Jenks, who turned away from the window to sit in the jump seats behind the pilot and fiddle with his belt.

'Oh, right then, everybody hold on to something. Here we go!' yelled Reece.

They fell out of the sky and landed on a roof beside some other planes. 'By the drowned king,' Philip swore. 'You call that a landing!' shouted Philip as he flicked switches to open the plane door.

'There was no more fuel,' called back Reece.

'You are a better pilot than you are a liar,' Philip said before jumping out of the plane.

The rest of the crew followed, the other planes on the roof belonging to other teams varied in size, shape and colour. Some looking more like insects or birds with many wings than like ships. Their own ship, the Redfish, looked like the drawing of a sea serpent found on the old human maps but as magnificent as she was, she was still a modest ship and smaller than most of the ships on the roof. Mainly grey and with some red plating and some rust, she was their Redfish.

Philip was talking to what looked like the head of the base by the robes he wore but Ali was not sure till he introduce himself. 'Good night all, I am Madoff, the leader of the base,' and he shook all of their hands in the traditional way of the sand spirit, one shake of the hand then one shake of the wrist. Ali had met a few sand spirits before but they still fascinated her with skin like sandpaper and some were known to have bodies largely made up of sand, their movements were flowing and flawless. When Ali withdrew her hand, she found it to be covered in sand but that was not the strangest part. A leader of a base would never have the time to shake hands with all the teams that would fly in and out of a base, in fact, in all the bases that Ali had stayed at, she rarely even saw a base leader. They were very high up in the order of command, normally the base keeper or third in command greeted teams.

Yuki looked puzzled too but Yuki had a curiosity about the size of her dog Rex, so decided not to dwell on it anymore since she would soon find out if Yuki looked that perplexed. Philip left with Madoff and the base keeper called Anna joined them. She was another sand spirit, she led them down from the roof and at the bottom of the stair she pointed right, 'That way are dorms and baths left is the hall and kitchen.' She then proceeded to lead them to their rooms. 'I am sorry that you will have to double up as we have a lot of people on base today.'

Ali and Yuki's room was the same as Reece and Jenks' with a bed on either side of the room with a window at the back wall and a small sink below it. There were rich blue walls and an orange stone floor, very simple and not much different from other bases.

'The bathrooms are just down from here and if you would like to follow me again, we can see if the cook is still cooking.' She turned and made no sound as she walked.

The corridor opened out into a massive hall with a high ceiling and an atrium in the middle with a shallow stone pool below. Leaves have blown in through the atrium to decorate the pool and sail around on the breeze that had carried them there. There were arched windows on three sides, the ceiling was painted

15

with the constellations and from the dark floor rose many dark wooden tables and chairs.

As they entered, everyone in the room turned to stare at them. 'Lovely,' muttered Yuki and patted Rex nervously on the head.

'Take any table you want if you find one.' Anna left them and headed for the kitchen. Finding one did prove problematic but they settled in beside another team who offered to share theirs. Most of the time, every team was happy to talk to one another and trade their stories but the room was oddly quiet. Something was off, Ali could feel it. By their uniform only the med officer and sense keeper from the other team wanted to talk to them.

'Hi, I am Diego, a med officer, where have you guys flown from?'

'China, just picking up some scrolls for the capital library and helping out the local council arrest a bunch of Fire Martins for setting human crop alit, nothing much, what about yourself?' Reece inclined his head toward them but before they could answer food arrived, four bowls of stew and berries with pillow leaf juice to wash it down. The juice was even severed in the traditional way with a whole pillow leaf flowing on top. The leaf was eaten first and the only thing to save you from its incredibly sweet taste was the berries that were too bitter to drink without the leaf.

Ali did not remember the mission the same way as Reece and Jenks did, certainly not because he was the one who treated Reece's burn wounds. Luckily for Reece, he was a Stone Skin, which protected him somewhat. Fire Martins can't create their own fire, unlike Fires Nixes so they must carry it with them in specially designed jars. Yuki froze the ground, making fuel unavailable, while Ali stole the fire's oxygen. Jenks made quick work of the land fires and extinguished the jar flames, stopping the Martins from creating any more.

'Oh well, we had a scroll mission too, meant to be flying to Nairobi tonight but after the news, capital says there are going to be no more night flights,' Diego whispered low.

'What's the news?' piped in Yuki, leaning across the table to hear the other team better.

'Where is your Capitan? Why have you not heard yet?' the sense exclaimed, her sign was a big green bird with a bronze beak who sat on the table with them, senses love to talk in questions but never really liked an answer. Their captain nearly always ate with them, if he was not in the hall talking to a friend or another team captain.

'We only arrived just now,' replied Ali, to break the cycle of questions that would go on.

Diego cleared his throat, 'Well, you were going to hear sooner or later, a ship just went down over the southern ocean and people are saying it was not an accident.' Ships crashing was rarely a fault with the ship or bad weather but something like this was unheard of. *Well, that explained the mood in the room*, Ali thought.

Yuki took in a breath deeply to ready herself for the hundred questions she was about to let loose, but nobody could answer the who, what, where and when. Diego looked sad and said that it was early days and that everyone was in the dark. After hearing that, no one spoke for the rest of their meal, lost in their own thoughts.

Ali and Yuki left the hall together as Reece and Jenks stayed to see if they could get seconds but none was to be found, so they caught up easily. Just before the stairs to the roof, a team came down and blocked their path but they weren't plain Atlantis guardians, no, they were a shadow team. Teams were never hostile towards one another but this team was giving off unfriendly vibes and the corridor, to Ali, felt smaller than before. 'A bunch of green hands,' one of them said and the rest just stared. They fled past them to their rooms, the shadow never talked but these guys were definitely pushing their superiority. They were young as a team, Yuki and she had only been flying with them two seasons and she could not remember how long Reece and Jenks had been flying before they all became a team under Captain Philip. Though it had always been a common practice to mix green hands with older hands for better training but it would not be long before they would graduate and become full guardians.

Ali and Yuki had got to their rooms, Ali was just about to close the door when Yuki, who was sitting on her bed and jumped right off again, 'Let's go outside.'

Ali was not sure, especially with recent news and was nervous about a new place too but the fresh air and walk applied to her more. They left the boys to get an early night and slipped off base. There was no real need to sneak about the place as bases never had a curfew with guardians flying in and out at all times but they did not want to meet their captain.

Walking down the human streets was strange, there was no magic there. Yuki was a Frostnar with strong ice powers. While she looked human, she had no human blood and Rex had spells cast over him to protect him from human sight.

While Ali herself was a Sylph, she had some human blood in her family from generations back. Their captain was half Sylph, half leaf Nix. The only difference between them and humans was magic. With the curse of the Drowned King, humans lost all abilities to sense magic. The last king of Atlantis wanted more power, more control so he took the human's magic. So instead of controlling them, he lost them and lost control of the power. Some say it was the Gods who struck down Atlantis, maybe it was human greed that swallowed it.

Objects or places of pure magic like their ships are hidden or can be hidden by spells. Then there is hiding in plain sight, this is called the chameleon effect. Something may maintain its shapes like an office block or house but its true colours were hidden. So that office block might be a mall. Tonight, a flickering streetlamp half-illuminated, stairs lead up from the footpath. The upper floors of the bookshop were magically sealed. They found a dark corner in the back of a fairy café called the Golden Cauldron. The loud streets full of people and cars became a distant hum through the music and smells of the café. The room was hazy with colourful smoke as small black cauldrons bubbled at the centre of each table. A bit of home cooking was they needed, the bases food was always great but they needed something that wasn't exactly healthy. Plus, they could order some Rex friendly treats and water too. The talk soon turned to the crashed plane, to be honest, Ali's mind had not left the news since hearing it.

'It could have been human, you know,' Yuki edged quietly, breaking away from her dessert, a honey cake. Ali had finished her forest berry cake far too quickly and ladled more tea from the cauldron into her cup.

'But how is that possible? Humans can't detect our planes,' Ali whispered.

'Well, human technology has been advancing rapidly lately and they could have invented something new.'

'You know that nothing can come close to magic and they can't smell it, hear it or see it.'

'Ah, but can they taste it?'

'I don't know, why don't you ask.'

'If I could, I would,' said Yuki and leaned back in her chair, clearly full and petted Rex. Ali always thought that out of them both, it should have been Yuki who could have been a Halfling, she would love to talk to them. They could see her if she was one of them through the tiny amount of DNA they shared.

Ali paid with Atlantis coin but they always carried some human money, which they learned that it was good to keep some on them from the past experiences. They then separately ordered more food to take home with them. Another thing learned was that if they went out, they have to bring Reece and Jenks a little something to keep them happy. Carrying the parcels back was thankfully uneventful, though Yuki did bring up the time when they ran into trouble, they were coming back from one of their city explorations when a group of humans stopped them and demanded Ali's wallet, of course, they did not see Yuki or Rex. So Ali had nothing to fear but they could not use their magic on humans. So Ali threw the wallet at them and ran away from the unpleasant happening and they now tried to keep out of them.

Ali woke up that morning to find the bed opposite her was empty and Rex was also gone. 'Damn it!' Ali flung back the covers and put on clothes as quickly as she could without putting any hole in them that should not be there.

'Where in the underworld could she be?' Yuki always woke her up before leaving or sometimes it was Yuki who couldn't get out of the bed. Clothes on and bag packed, she went next door and knocked on Jenks and Reece's room.

'Come in,' called Jenks, Ali stepped into the room. Jenks was sitting up in the bed, reading a book and Reece, by the looks of it, was still deeply asleep, his Babylon lantern burning.

'Have you seen Yuki?' She open the curtains and Reece moaned, turning in the bed.

'Not since you and her left the food last night. Why?'

'I think we should get going soon,' she said, stealing Recce's pillow from under his head.

Reece turned again but this time fell out of the bed, 'what did you say?' He picked himself up.

'It's time to leave,' laughing Jenks and closed his book. 'I got to return this to the library here and I will be right up.'

'Okay, I will go find Yuki,' Ali said while opening the door to leave their room.

'Is there any time for breakfast?'

'No,' said Jenks and Ali together.

Ali slung her bag over her shoulder and walked quickly down to the hall and just as she round the corner and nearly bumped smack into Diego the med from last night, 'Oh sorry, I have you seen Yuki?'

'Yes, sure, she is at the table with Vialla.'

The two sense keepers were immersed in conversion and did not hear her coming till Rex gave a low friendly growl, he sound more like a toad than the oversized chameleon dog he was, Yuki looked up at the sound. 'Good morning,' she smiled, 'I got some news for you.'

'Well, you can tell me on the way we have to go,' Ali smiled at Vialla and then gave a prompting poke to Yuki to get her out of her chair.

'Okay, Vialla, hopefully, we will run into each other soon.' They left the hall and went to get Yuki's bag in the room while packing, Yuki shared her news. 'I heard that this morning the captain spent the whole night up talking with the leader.'

'And who told you this?' Ali asked, sitting down on the bed heavily.

'The cook said they ordered dinner at three in the morning and poor Bennie has been up all night.' Yuki always tried to befriend the cooks, while most people fear being buried alive or drowning, Yuki feared being poised.

'Maybe they are old friends,' Ali countered.

Yuki turned from her packing to her, 'Maybe.'

A knock on their door sounded. 'Ya?' called Ali.

Jenks leaned in around the door. 'Reece is getting the ship ready. Are you two good to go, then?' Jenks queried. They walked up to the roof where the ship was fuelled and waiting. The captain was talking to the leader of the base. Ali and Yuki stayed quiet when passing and bored the Redfish.

A few minutes later, the captain climbed on and said, 'Straight to Atlantis, Reece, as fast as we can.'

Chapter 2
Atlantis

The plane circled the city, the broken heart of their world, once before landing on a small island just off its main shores. Atlantis, the oldest and most beautiful city in the world, yet all that remained was the central island with its three pale stone spires and a ring of smaller islands beyond those and in between were islets, the tops of old towers severing as sentries. The first sentries that had surrounded the city in older days were sunken and no more than rocks at the surface of the water, coral grew where there were once gardens. Where the water was shallow, ruins could be seen in the turquoise colours. A dark blue hole to the south of the island marked the water, deeper used be to the Colosseum of Atlantis, where the great duels of old were held and still were in a different fashion.

Most of Atlantis lay under the waves. It was said to be haunted. The new underwater city to the southeast with only one used road passing from the city through the ruins and under the temple. A pool at the surface level of the temple connected Merfolk to the dry levels but that was only for Merfolk councillors. All other Merfolk come ashore at the docks or Islands avoiding the ruins. *Maybe it was only memories that lived there now. Someone else's memories and stories,* Ali thought. Some say it was after the ice age when the sea rose higher than before and drown Atlantis. Others said it was the gods who grew jealous and set the sea against them, even the humans know of that story, passing on the terrors of that day and night. Their legend was a reality they all lived with. She always tried to picture Atlantis before the drowning but she felt she could not stretch her imagination far enough.

The only other people who lived there full time were the high council of Atlantis. There were meant to be a High Guard when they were not travelling for missions and The Line of six people, who looked after the last of Atlantis and kept the old traditions alive.

The base keeper of the island was a selkie you could tell because sometimes they can't hide their seal whiskers. 'Good day to you all,' he smiled, his whiskers moving as he talked. 'There is a gathering in the temple.' The temple was really no temple at all. It was the greatest tower on the centre island, the seat of the Atlantis high counsel.

'Thank you, when does it start?' Captain Philip asked.

'An hour or so, captain, they have been waiting for you.'

'Ali, Yuki, you two take the orb to the library, Reece and Jenks with me,' Captain Philip ordered.

They left them to take care of themselves, heading straight to the temple. Ali and Yuki climbed back on the Redfish and collected the orbs from the ship's safe. Only the crew of the ship or a high scribe could open the safe. Ali placed her hand on the safe and blue vein spend out from where her hand touched the black metal, the door opened when the blue veins reached the hinges. Inside, there was one wooden chest and Ali opened it to check on the orb. It was glowing alive with knowledge, spells, or memories. The size of orbs could vary from an apple up to a football, they never faded the perfect vessel for a century of storage. They only had one orb today, which was unusual. Guardians carried back-and-forth orbs everywhere so all knowledge was shared, expanded, and collected. Ali gently placed the blue and silver swirling orb into a wooden chest. They were difficult to make and impossible to fix.

Ali put the chest under her arm and they walked the short distance to the shore. *The council has been waiting on the captain, something serious must be going on*, thought Ali. They made their way onto a wooden jetty. There was no bridge connecting this island to the centre island. Though it was connected to the more important islands, like the lead shadow base had bridges to the main island. They took a small boat of their choosing. Yuki turned the compass's north at the head of the boat to face the centre island and the boat started up, taking them to another jetty on the other side.

'Do you think it started with that base keeper back in Athens?' Ali asked.

'I know for a fact it started. Rex told me that it did start with him.'

Animals have much stronger senses than us and the link that Yuki and Rex had allowed her to pick up on things that's only Rex would know. Yuki was right, Ali agreed that there was something wrong with the captain.

They climbed out of the boat and headed towards the library, the three buildings formed a semi-circle, which opened out onto a huge stone square. The library was the left of the temple, which was the council house plus court and opposite the Volts, which housed the bank and administration of Atlantis. Ali saw no one around. *They all must be in the temple*, she thought, *that can't be a good sign*. The place was beginning to look like the desolate drowned city of legend, when someone appeared out of the library and sat down on the steps in front. Whoever it was paid them no mind but they looked as worried as Ali felt. As they came closer, he turned his attention toward them. Ali couldn't believe it was Samdar Rowan, the high scribe of Atlantis, just sitting on the steps. His ancestors could be traced back to the birth of Atlantis as orb casters, though no one makes them on Atlantis anymore. Ali had only seen him from afar in the library when she had been on other scroll missions. Samdar smiled at them, 'Is that an orb for me?'

'Yes, from China,' Ali replied, a little flustered to be talking to one of the top people of Atlantis.

'Ah yes, I have been expecting something from there for some time. Right, we better bring it inside and have a look,' he said, rising from the steps.

Ali and Yuki nodded, Ali thought that they were both too shocked to be speaking with the high scribe of Atlantis to actually say anything. They followed him inside to the hall of the library. There was a glass dome where all the levels in the library opened in the cavernous space. Ali never thought she would see the library empty but there were only the three of them in that great space. 'Where is everyone?' she asked Samdar.

'They are in the temple for a private meeting but everyone has a look.' Samdar rolled his eyes. 'Too small an island for secrets.'

Ali looked at Yuki, *this really can't be good*, she thought. Samdar stopped a massive ancient oak desk, it looked like a fallen tree in a forest just the top was smoothed flat. Maybe it fell out of a book, Ali had mused often before or some kind of magic was involved because the hulking piece of furniture still was growing leaves on it. Samdar picked a logbook that lay open on the desk, 'I see every orb, scroll, book, stone and scrap of paper that comes and goes through those door ladies but there is no time for me to read them all as I would like to.' He seemed sad like it was shameful that he had not read every book in the library.

Yuki smiled at him, 'It would take a few lifetimes to read everything here.'

'You are right but then I would need infinity to keep up with what will be written in the futures to come.'

They climbed the stairs to the fifth level, passing rows on rows of bookshelves, then Samdar started muttering himself. He then stopped so suddenly that Ali almost dropped the chest when she walked into the back of him.

'Ah, here we are,' announced Samdar, turning left down a row and turned right and left again. They went so far into the library they could no longer see the dome overhead. 'We are nearly there,' he assured. 'Sometimes I get lost in here but that's the way my mind works. I can remember a story and dates but have a terrible sense of direction.'

They stopped in front of a row but instead of having shelves, it had hundreds of little doors varying in sizes. Samdar opened a door using his handprint Ali held out the chest which he opened and placed the orb inside and said, 'This orb is very old and is missing its twin.'

'How can an orb have a twin?' Ali said, confused, never coming across this in her study.

Samdar closed the little door. 'Well if they contain information like if one held a curse the twin would hold the cure if one held the question the other the answer and the question is just as important or else we don't really know the answer.'

'What does that orb hold?' Ali asked, now anxious to know what she had been carrying so close to her, keeping it safe.

'I have no idea what it is. Some orbs will only give up their secrets in the presence of their twin and I also don't know where the twin is but whatever it is, it better to have one safe with us.'

On the way back Yuki asked Samdar, 'why aren't you in the temple?'

'Well, no one would catch me reading when I'm meant to be working but the temple is where bad tiding lives plus the young scribes gossip enough for me know what's going on everywhere,' he sighed.

'The bringing of twins together is not common knowledge but I would trust two guardians of Atlantis. The orbs were made like that to keep them safe.'

'Well, we are not guardians yet. We still have to finish this season before we can graduate.'

'Oh dear.' said Samdar, 'well, I will just have to trust the both of you then.' Ali thought that he did not look worried at all, though.

'If you find that second orb, bring it back and we can see what secrets it has for us.' He left them on the second floor, muttering that he had been meaning to get to a book from there for months.

'Well, he is not so bad, is he?' Yuki said, loud enough for him to hear.

Ali nearly bashed her with the empty chest. 'He is not likely poor of hearing, you know,' she whispered.

They were outside at the top of the library steps when people started to pour out of the temple. Ali and Yuki stayed where they were, to see if they could find their team from their height. Neither of them nor Rex were fond of crowds and not this crowd, who was angry and sullen, some even shouting.

'Excuse me,' called a man running up the steps, taking two at a time. Ali and Yuki stepped aside and the man dived through the gap in the library doors.

'Wow, someone is in a hurry.' Ali raised her eyes brows.

'That was Samar, Samdar's grandson, his parents are orb casters.' said Yuki, craning her neck back for a view through the library door. 'Rumour is Samdar is retiring.'

Reece came bounding up the steps out of breath as he reached them. 'The captain's brother has been killed in the crash!' Reece exclaimed.

Yuki gasped, covering her mouth with a hand. It did not register with Ali for a few seconds, her mind going completely blank with the shock.

'They knew it was his ship, the Two Tails, last night but they did not know for sure if the crew survived but teams went to the crash site. There is going to be an investigation. When they the pull up the ship and bring it back here.' Reece puffed.

'How is the captain?' asked Ali. Yuki was on the brink of tears and Rex tried to nuzzle her for comfort. Ray was Philip's only brother and his parents were gone long ago now. Ali couldn't imagine what he was going through.

'He was silent, the High Council offered him their condolences and leave till the investigation was over but he refused it. There will be a funeral in a few weeks when they bring back the bodies.'

'Where is he now?' Ali wanted to know.

'He has gone to the Volts to pick the next mission, he says we are to be back at the ship and really to leave.'

'Were you with him when he found out?' said Yuki, trying to hold back a sob.

'No, the council took him and a few others relayed to the other crew aside telling them the news first, then the council came out and announced it to everyone gathered.'

'The Line is holding prays in the temple now but the captain is refusing to go.'

'They also said that they don't know if it was foul play or a fault with the ship but they are suspicious, saying if it was friendly fire those who held apart would be severely punished.'

As they walked down the step, they were passed by dozens of scribes, all talking of the gathering. *Poor Samdar thought no peace for him and now no peace for the captain*, Ali thought gloomily.

By the time they got to the dock all the fastest boats were gone, leaving this small wooden boat that chugged along the water, looking up they could see that many ships had already taken flight the rising vertically off the islands and turning when they reached a height they turned flying at speed. One or two ships had come low over the sea and disturbing the water rocking their boat a little harder. *The sky had no right to be that blue*, thought Ali as they drew closer to the other side.

Chapter 3

Mission

Some humans call this the end of the world and did have that feeling. If the world was flat, the southern ocean would have been on its edge.

'I can't believe this is the last mission and then graduation,' Ali gushed as they came into land at Lumast Base. This was true the season was almost at its end as navigator she had to train with the team for three seasons, a sense keeper three and the pilot and the medical officer both four seasons, then anyone with those three pieces of training could go to become a captain if they wanted. The captain bit was just a daydream for Ali though but now she tried to focus on the mission or there won't be a navigator now or a captain in the future.

'Hey you don't want to jinx it, this is the last mission,' Reece joked.

'They don't judge you on the last mission alone,' Yuki argued back, 'and no one knows how you passed your test.'

This was also true but Ali did not want to join in the fight. She was nervous. This was quite a long mission, they had to visit two temples and join security forces at a festival. The Future Mists or The Mist and Fire was an international festival, the third biggest event after the summer and winter solstice in the year. It was so important that The Line left Atlantis to oversee the tradition with Arcwqil Dareghn leading, the role is for life so they took turns in being head of The Line. It was Ali's first time attending, well, the first time that she would remember her mother brought her when she was four or five, plus her brother Emanuel and younger sister Mia. She vaguely remembered a volcano and fireworks. The others recounted tales from their personal visits, duelling, food, the offering of wishes and doubts to the volcano. But everyone talked of the walk from wishing volcano Xerhina, which roughly translates to 'blood of the sun' in the local language to the higher to but sleeping volcano Okowazira, which means the mist that whispers. This walk and these volcanoes are at the centre of the festival and a most important pilgrimage for many people.

They had one day before the festival and two days before they had to fly back. Usually, teams that had green hands stopped before the end of the season so they could go home, prepare, and be with family before they graduated.

They stopped their fighting when the captain came down from his office. 'Cap, why are we picking up two orbs? There are loads of other teams here,' asked Jenks.

'They are all here for the festival and none of them are flying back as soon as we are,' he answered. 'Right, the lot of you better check-in and meet me in the hall when you are done,' he ordered, opening the door and jumping out.

'That the most he has said to us since we left,' mused Yuki, staring after the captain.

'He never talked that much anyway,' yawned Reece.

'I know but this is different,' stated Yuki.

Jenks cleared his throat, 'It is to be expected.'

Ali only nodded in agreement with Jenks.

Rex growled at the opened door as a man poked his head through, 'Hello! Are you lot ready? We don't have all day so many people come and go and no time to sit in their planes.'

They all mumbled an apology and followed him out. They flew all night, Ali blinked at the brightness of the sun, which was still on the horizon but the yard that they had landed was busy with people making preparations. There were boxes of strange food and colourful tents.

They followed the base keeper who was a Leaf Nix, the grass in the yard seem to grow greener where he walked or stood. Inside the base, he told that there was no room for them so they would have to sleep on the Redfish. He showed them the baths, then finally the kitchen beside the hall where he left them in a hurry.

They saw Phillip talking to a woman, she was a tall Fire Nix. Ali had been around Fire Nixes but none or even Jenks could claim that their hair looked like actual fire. The captain called them over and when the woman turned her red eyes on them, Ali could feel the heat on her skin that the woman radiated.

'Everyone, this is Kara, she will be your guide. There are shields around both temples so no planes can fly in, so we will have to split up and go on foot. Ali,

Yuki and Jenks, you are to go with Kara to the upper temple and Reece, you are with me to the isle temple.'

'If I don't see you tonight, I will see you tomorrow morning. Right Reece, we have a boat to catch.' the captain left and Reece with him.

They turned to face Kara, 'I see you have met James. He runs everything around here, now we are very busy so we better get out of his way and I will learn names on the way.'

She led them outside to a large grey bird-like ship with orange panels. 'I thought we weren't allowed to fly into the place?' Ali asked, confused now.

'We are not allowed within a thirty-mile radius of the temple but it takes a long time to get to that boundary.' She opened the door and let them in first. She jumped into the pilot seat and took off so fast that Ali felt gravity pushing against her chest. 'We will be there in a few hours,' Kara explained as she started the ship. Ali replied with nothing. She was finding it hard to breathe so talking was passed her and the others.

'What are your names again?' She yelled over the roar of the engine, whatever it ran on, it was more than charge and water. Ali didn't know ships could fly this fast. After a moment or two, she had gained control of her breathing.

'I am Ali,' she told Kara.

Kara turned in her chair. 'Ah, one of them speaks but it's a Sylph, the air belongs to you and you to it so what do you think of my ship?' she grinned.

Yuki's nails dug holes in the arm of her chair and Rex had his claws out to keep him fixed to the floor. He moved to sit closer to Yuki and Ali could see that he had left holes too. Jenks was not looking much better either, he closed his eyes and moaned, 'I think am going to throw up.'

'Oh, please don't, there are bags under your seat.'

Jenks rummaged around under his seat with one hand over his mouth. He pulled out a tray and brown bags flew everywhere. Kara levelled the ship. 'Sorry but we must keep the speed, the temple does not accept visitors after night or as they oafishly put, none enter under the star's eyes.' Yuki tried to comfort him but it was doubtful that he heard above the hum of the engine and his own retching.

'We are closer to the temple than the base soon and they have the best healers this side of the mountain,' hollered Kara back who was now missing her brassy tone. 'But still, it's a pleasure to have you all on board.'

'I don't think Jenks would agree with you,' she mused.

'Are you working at the festival?' Yuki asked Kara.

'Yes, as a fire ward, the festival has so many fires that they need people just to look after them alone.'

'So is the Mists Festival, you have worked there before?' Kara asked them when they said 'No' she smiled, 'It's still enjoyable, just take part in a different way.'

The future Mists Festival was nearly 700 years old. It started with a group of people who believed a god dwelt in the mountain, a god of smoke and no fire, he would tell them their futures. Now the mountain smokes no more but now people come from all over the world to look into the lake at the top to see the unknown.

'I remember my first Mist working, 50 years ago now and Xerhina who is always restless that so many Fire Nix's need to monitor it and keeping people safe is a full-time job any other time of the year but the festival always brings more people. Well, that was the year that Xerhina had to erupt,' she sighed, thinking about the memory. 'It took 400 Fire Nix's and other magic to control the eruption, which was small for Xerhina. We guided the lava down one side of the mountain. This is why the festival does not surround the Twin Mountains anymore. The ash cloud was immense, erupting miles into the sky. We needed over 300 Sylphs to stop ash raining downing. Together, we had control until everyone was clear of the eruption zone. We lost a lot of people that day and the festivals after that always hold prayer for that day.' Ali could tell the memory was still painful for Kara.

'My mother was there that day,' shared Jenks. 'She and my family tried to help.'

'A lot of people did but there is no fighting a volcano. It was not first or the last time for Xerhina.'

Three hours later, they landed at a wooden cottage shaded under trees in the forest glade. Kara jumped out and shouted, 'I will bring the trunk around.' A few moments later, Ali heard this rumbling sound and Kara parked the strangest looking trunk alongside the plane. The trunk didn't have wheels but it made up for that with many metal legs, then the rest of the body was more grey metal and glass.

'Don't worry, the gatekeeper said I could borrow it till we get to the next house.'

'How far is that?' queried Ali.

'A couple of miles but we will make it in good time in the beast.'

'Is that what you call it? It looks more like cricket to me.' Yuki eyed the beast with suspicion.

'Nah, she doesn't jump.' Kara smiled.

'Small mercies,' muttered Jenks. 'Some med can't even treat travel sickness.'

Ali turned back to the plane, finding it hard to take her eyes off the beast. Yuki had Jenks by the arm and was helping him down the steps.

'How are you feeling now, Jenks?' asked Ali.

'I know it's not like me,' he sighed gloomily. 'I think I am a little stressed at the moment about work.'

'Hey, it's okay to feel that maybe the sickness is part of being a bit stressed out,' Ali figured, trying her best to sound cheerful cause she knew how he felt.

'I feel a bit down,' Yuki admitted, squeezing his arm, 'but we got each other.'

They both then sat up in the front with Kara while Jenks lay down in the back with Rex. She turn the engine on and the legs of the beast grew. They were now nearly as tall as the ship. They entered the jungle at the base of the hill and the beast started its climb. They were gently shaken from side to side.

'Better than wheels, they would get stuck and crush everything,' explained Kara as they entered the shaded world.

They came out of the jungle to the base of a grassy hill. 'We can go no farther. No metal can pass at this point if you have anything, metal keys, gadgets, jewellery, you must leave them or you will not pass.'

'I am not sure about this mission,' Yuki said, worried, looking down at her hands and all rings she wore.

'Why do you wear so many rings?' asked Kara.

'Well, they all have a meaning and were given to me at a certain point in my life. It's Frostnar tradition and culture but really I don't have that many.' Yuki explained.

Most of the Frostnar wore rings and those rings told that person's life story. The first ring they receive is the Ever frost ring, it was for their people, the second ring is the stone and the third is grass, they are symbols of the earth and would break also at the person's death meaning that the person had returned to the earth. Yuki was allowed to keep these three and a glass one the rest were bronze, silver or another metal.

'I have never taken these rings off since the day I got them,' Yuki declared, who was twisting a Silver ring around her finger. Ali knew that ring was a family ring, it had cuts in it to mark out her family members.

She knew that it was a very serious thing to remove those rings. Yuki had once said that the Frostnar believed that one would forget their life if they did not wear their rings. Ali would go alone. Jenks was too sick to go and Yuki could not part with her rings. Ali took off her watch and a necklace with a feather pendant, a Sylph sign her mother had given her, handing them to Jenks, who popped them into his top jacket pocket. 'I will keep them safe,' he promised, tapping the pocket.

'I will stay here with Jenks and Yuki until you send down a healer,' said Kara. 'Just follow the stone steps up to the top, if you are lucky you might meet the temple leader, he is a bit of seer.'

Ali looked back as she climbed to see Jenks climbing out of the beast to vomit on the grass and she hurried on. The stone steps were worn in the places where everyone before had stepped on the same part of the step.

She reached the top out of breath, which was too many stairs and found a man waiting for them under the gateway arch. 'You are from Atlantis, are you not?' the man said.

'Yes, I am and I have a friend at the bottom of the hill who needs a healer.'

'Why does he need a healer?'

'He does not fly very well,' said Ali.

'I will see what our healer can do for him, come this way for the scroll.'

He led her through the gate and into a yard circled by wooded buildings which were covered in ornately carved animals on top of every steeply pitched roof. There were wind vanes too but they all pointed in different directions. 'Wait here a moment.' Her guide disappeared into the largest building, a temple.

Ali heard voices from beyond the circle. She left the buildings, following the voices. Walking through a grassy field, Ali came to a workshop on the edge of the cliff. A woman held a ball of fire and another woman held a leaf from which she weaved magic around and placed it into the ball of fire. Then the fireball was tossed high into the air spinning, the two women worked in harmony layering magic and protective spells. A green swirling orb floated to the ground, it rolled a little before one of the women scooped it up.

'Excuse me,' coughed Ali's guide.

32

Ali turned sheepishly, 'Sorry, I have only ever seen orb creation in textbooks.'

The man nodded, 'A rare craft today, even the sandpit method is dying out, most are done in metal moulds in factories. Are you ready?'

'Yes,' Ali replied and followed the man back to the temple. 'What are they making these orbs on?'

'We are studying botany here and we hope to share what we find, now here we are, this is where you will find what you are looking for,' he nodded, leaving her back in front of the temple.

Ali had to use her power to push open the heavy wooden door, it was dim inside and the air was thick with smoke. Ali would have missed the temple master if he did not call out to her. 'Who is there?'

'Hello, I hale from Atlantis, I am here to collect a scroll,' she convened.

The man didn't look up from a desk covered in stacks of books. 'When will you travel back?'

'The scroll will travel to Atlantis in the next couple of days.'

'It is a shame it will not get there quicker. Are you sure there is no ship that travels sooner?'

'I am not sure, everyone is tied up at the festival.'

He nodded, 'Fair enough. I believe you were meant to have companions and so for your troubles, I will answer two questions.'

He rose from his chair and he walked across the hall to a small alcove with shelves and chests. He used a ladder to pick out a chest near the top and handed it down to Ali, 'What are your questions?'

Ali looked at him, confused, then realising dawned that he was a seer. Questions, she had lots of those about many things but these questions were being offered like reward and a wise man got to have answers. 'Why can't metal come up the hill?' Ali asked for a basic first, she thought.

'Metal is natural but not how we shape it and use it. The hill knows and the hill knows all on the hill and you, what else will you ask of me?'

'What happened to the guardian ship that when down?'

'That is a question that I asked myself but I think you will find out soon.'

Ali said goodbye and thank you.

The man replied with a nod and returned to his desk.

Ali closed the door behind her. No power needed, she walked through the empty temple grounds slowly taking in the strange buildings.

Everyone was sitting on the grass when Ali returned but Kara had stepped away to talk to a man Ali could only presume was the healer.

'Did you get the scroll?' asked Jenks.

'Yes, how do you feel?' Untucking the scroll from her robe.

'Good, the healer gave me a potion to drink and some extra to take later, it did not taste too bad either, how was the temple then?'

'Beautiful looking, defiantly worth climbing the stairs to get there too and the master offered to answer questions.' Ali stretched and relayed the answers.

'He might have been right about something though, when I was in the Volts back on Atlantis, I heard the people who gave out the mission talking. They said that the captain should not be sent anywhere south of the equator. The captain swapped his mission for this mission. We are not meant to be here but the captain might get the answer he looking for.'

Chapter 4

Feast and Fest

They arrived back at the base before dark fell and a cool-mist rose. 'Alright, you lot get some rest, the star's eyes are nearly out,' Kara pressed as she brought the ship into Lumast base. Kara confirmed, 'I will most likely see you tomorrow up on the mountain.'

'Okay, we see tomorrow,' Ali replied.

'Thank you for your help,' Yuki nodded.

'Anytime,' Kara smiled and patted Jenks on the shoulder before leaving them.

Ali handed the scroll over to Jenks, who was going back to the empty plane to get an early night. She was also tired, it had been a strange day but still, she wanted to find Reece before going to bed and she knew Yuki would feel the same way. They searched the whole base and even asked a few people but the base was so busy that no one knew where anybody was.

In the end, they gave up after half an hour retreating to bed and that's when they found him, sitting up in his bunk talking to Jenks.

'Ah Jenks, why didn't you tell us that he was here?' exclaimed Yuki, folding her arms.

'I was too comfortable,' said Jenks and sinking lower into his bunk.

'Where is the captain?' Asked Ali.

'He is at a meeting on base with other caps, it's about the festival tomorrow,' said Reece, who began to fluff up his pillow.

'You know we are not meant to be here, the captain was not meant to take any mission near the southern ocean, you know too close to the crime and the personal connection thing,' said Yuki.

'I know Jenks was telling me and I think the man you were talking to in the temple is right when the captain and I landed at the island temple. He left me to collect the scroll. Then I remember that the temple was the first to pick up a distress call from the ship.'

'The captain is looking for answers himself,' said Ali.

'He will get them too, I did some sneaking about and found that the recovery mission of the ship is being launched from that island.' Reece muffled as he let his head hit the pillow.

No one said anything for a few minutes, all their minds on the same man. Ali cleared her throat, which seemed to have dried up considerably. 'When is the recovery mission planned for?' she asked Reece.

'The day after the festival,' said Reece and he sat up straight in his bed.

'Is he going to take us with or leave us behind?' Yuki speculated.

'I really don't know but I know that any of the teams going out there would not be allowed to take him along. The Atlantis high council forbid any relatives or friends to take part in the recovery or the inquiry, which only makes sense really but I think the captain might not be listening to sense right now,' said Reece. 'He has got the basis for flying the redfish but it will take more than to get out here plus the navigation calculations.'

Ali did not sleep as well as she would have liked to and when she woke everyone was gone, except for Rex, who had taken Jenks' bunk that made her smile. Jenks hated dog hairs in his bed and he always made a big deal of how long it took him to clean. She got dressed quickly and knelt down to give Rex a pet but he jumped off the bed before she could and he swanned out the door with his tail high in the air. This usually was a sign to follow him.

The team was sitting outside under the plane wing on some folding chairs. Rex stopped and curled up in a ball beside Yuki. The sun was just climbing over the mountains and Ali could already feel its heat. It was going to be a sweltering day. 'Good morning, any sign of the captain yet?' she asked.

'No, not since yesterday,' said Reece, 'there is another chair behind Jenks if you want to join us.'

'Thanks.' She picked up a box and let it drop for it to fold out. Yuki handed over her a box of fruit. She took an apple and handed the box to Jenks.

'Most of the teams are already up on the mountain and all the tents were put up yesterday so I am not too sure as to what we will be doing,' shrugged Jenks.

Well, that explained why the yard was so quiet, thought Ali. 'So does anyone know what this festival is going to be like?'

'Well, a man came around earlier handing everyone a map of the mountain,' said Yuki, and passed her one from the stack she had pinned under a glass bottle of water.

The map showed a bird's-eye view of the mountain with different symbols marking out the different tents. It would be good to know where things were so she folded up the map and put it in her pocket. Plus, the map would be a souvenir from today, another one to add to the map collection. You had to be obsessed with geography and maps to be a navigator.

Rex made a mumbling sound and they all looked around to see the captain striding across the yard. He seemed pale and tired around the eyes than the last time Ali had seen him.

'I don't care where you got those chairs, just get rid of them and be quick about it. I don't want to be the last team leaving here,' Philip said and walked past and climbed onto the plane without another word.

'They belong to the base,' said Reece but the captain had gone so he pushed his chair backwards to let it fall and fold back into a box and they stacked them back against the base wall.

They were all on the plane with Reece and were just starting to take off when Jenks asked the captain, 'What will we be doing at the festival?'

'Security, there is nothing to it. You just had to maintain your presence and make sure everyone is alright. We are not the real security, we are just the backup, so keep radios on at all times. If anything happens, you contact base,' Philip ordered, turning to his office.

'I will bring a med bag then,' said Jenks, and started to sort through a bag of medical supplies.

They reached the mountain later in the morning than the captain would have liked. 'Right, we are late but there is no point in dwelling on it, you have patrols for the rest of the day and at nine o'clock you have to make your way to the top that's where the main event is happening at midnight but there is a ceremony beforehand which nearly everyone will be at. Then be back at the plane when it is over.' He turned and left.

Ali felt uneasy as guardians they would do all kinds of work but she had to do anything like crowd control. It was not like they were going to blend into the crowd either; they had to wear the Atlantis' grey and black uniforms. While the whole mountain had been turned into a multi-coloured firework of tents and people in clothes of every colour imaginable. There is singing and theatre at every corner. Dark descendants mock battling Atlantis, the oldest play in the world, still fighting it out all these centuries later.

Strange and delicious smells filled the air. Ali began to feel hungry but she knew that she would have nothing to worry about because nearly every third tent was selling a food from a different corner of the world. Ali had never seen much of it before and some of it still moved. She was sure what was inside the loaves of bread or pies to make them move but she did not really want to know either. They stopped at a stand selling vegetable stew and everyone got a little bowl. When they tried to pay the stand owner, he refused them, saying it is for free for Festival security and Atlantis Guardians.

They all said thank you in turn, Ali was tempted to ask for another bowl because it was so tasty but she knew better, her mother always told her to accept a gift with both hands, not with one because the other would fill with greed. She missed her mother, Emanuel, and Mia. She hoped there would be time to see them before graduation. It had been months since she had been home. Reece nudged her arm, jostling her from the daydream of home.

'There is duel tournament!' Reece exclaimed, enthusiastically pointing to a large wooden board with names, ages and symbols. Some of the teams represented their own countries some countries humans did not know of but these tended to be small islands or city-states that were easy to shroud, others represented themselves. Duel fighting could be as much a pastime as a profession, with teams winning money for every battle they part take in. There were torments at every major festival and the main holidays of the year, the winter and summer solstice. These were the two biggest torments, held in the underwater Colosseum of Atlantis.

The crowds began to thicken. A man who had been shouting out bets stopped when they passed him by. While it is not illegal but it was frowned upon to betting so close to the duelling arena and many of the teams were superstitious about having people betting the outcome of their fights close to them.

An amphitheatre sunken into the side of the mountain opened out in front of them, hundreds had already taken their seats on the stone steps. Ali saw other guardians near the base of the amphitheatre they would not be needed here, Ali would not have minded seeing a couple of rounds but she would have no say with Reece acting as team leader, he could make them walk all night but the Reece, Ali had come to know would never do such a thing. Reece dropped himself into a seat and stretched. 'I think we will take a break for an hour or so.' Reece turned his head up to the sun and smiled.

Jenks did not look pleased but sat down beside Reece without a word. Yuki sat on the other side of Reece. Yuki love duelling with Myron, Celeb and Kumari, her older brothers. They competed as a team together, they were quite high in the world rankings. It was Yuki who got her so interested in the world of duelling. Rex took up two seats beside her and closed his eyes. Looking around the weathered stone circle that must have been here since the festival began, Ali saw that other guardians in the crowd clearly had the same idea as Reece. Silence fell on the amphitheatre as a woman in flowing purple robes walked out into the centre of the arena, from there her voice carried easily.

'Hello and welcome to the five hundred and forty-seventh tournament at the festival of future mists. Good luck to all who step out to fight brave and fair. May they stay.' Her passionate voice echoed through the arena.

'Brave and fair, may they stay brave and fair,' the crowd roared back. Ali whispered it along with them but Yuki made up for her quietness by shouting the saying back. The lady in purple retreated and from opposite sides of the arena, the two teams of three stepped out. One of the teams wore red and were representing Peru. The other team from Malaysia wore blue. The three people on the team had their ages added together and whoever had the oldest combined age was allowed the first strike, this rule now had hospitals recording the time down the exact second in which a baby was born. The game touched everyone from around their world. It was just as important as art or politics, even their leader in Atlantis, Baron Lunglock, used to take part in his younger days. He was a Stone skin like Reece.

The Malaysian team was the oldest at one hundred and two and the young Peruvian team would strike second with a combined age of fifty-nine. The two teams stood six strides apart, the person who stood in the middle was the fighter and their teammates who stood on either side were the shields. The fighter can only attack the fighter of the other team, the duel is won when the shields can no longer protect their fighter and if the fighter tries to defend themselves from attack.

Three drumbeats rolled through the arena, Ali could feel the sound in her chest. The duel was about to begin. The Malaysia fighter slowly raised her hands above her head, then brought them down quickly and threw a spinning ball of fire at the Peruvian fighter. The Peruvian first shielded, using air, pushed the ball of fire back and away from his fighter, the second shield turned the fire into the water so it rained in the no man's lands between the teams.

Yuki leaned over, 'That was a weak start. If the Malaysian can have her magic turned, they must be testing to see what the young team has.'

'I think we are about to find out for ourselves,' Ali whispered back.

The earth in front of the Peruvian fighter began to shift and crack. It turned to liquid swirling and flowing, then almost boiling when a creature crawled out, still taking the form as it walked up and down the arena, growing larger. Finally, it stood facing its creator, a giant jaguar. Creating the great beast from clay and holding this form must have taken a lot of energy as even from their far off seats Ali could see the Peruvian fighter shaking with eyes closed and face twisted in concentration.

The animal slowly turned in a wide circle to align himself with the enemy, leaving trenches on the earth where claws had been. He closed his open maw to let out a low, throaty growl.

Ali was in awe, she found it hard to pull her eyes away from the animal that had been formed from nothing but a man's imagination and the ground in front of him. She wanted to see the other team's faces, were they nervous, worried or even scared. When Ali finally ripped her eyes away from the cat, she could only see three duellers standing there looking very calm but also very still as if they moved, the cat would find them or maybe they were preparing with deep breathing. The Peruvian fighter still had his eyes closed so Ali presumed that he could see through the eyes of the jaguar. The cat put one paw forward, he could easily cross the space between the teams in the two bounds.

The two shield players on either side of the Malaysian fighter began to chant. The jaguar stepped closer, they chanted faster, shouting at this point, the jaguar leapt for the fighter as if sensing that to let the chant finish would be to meet his end. Pronounced claws flew through the air, their aim true to strike for victory, but suddenly wings blocked the way, two great birds materialised from rippling air in front of the shields, beating wings spread in front of their fighter. The jaguar fell back in shock and hissed at the now screeching birds, he made to strike them but they flew out of reach. The bird with blue and orange feathers hovered above the Malaysian team while the bird with glossy green feathers circled the sky above the jaguar. The orange and blue bird opened its beak to spit fire and ice at the cat but he sidestepped all as if they were puddles and he simply did not want to get his feet wet. Ali breathes a sigh of relief that she did not know she had been holding for the cat, she had thought the cat was finished when that bird opened its beak.

The orange and blue birds landed on the ground in front of their team, one shield nodded to the other, looks like it was time to introduce the green bird to the battlefield. The green bird drove at the cat, the screeching bird's call changed, it became louder and higher, Ali thought her ears were going to start bleeding but the sound seems to have a different effect on the cat he was pinned to the ground as if the sound was holding him down, the bird swooped down closer enough to touch the cat but it did not, it returned to the higher air to repeat the drive and the call again.

On the third drive, the jaguar can no longer rise, Ali leaned over to Yuki, 'What is happening to him?'

Yuki glanced at her before bringing her eyes back to the game, 'The bird is calling the jaguar back to the earth.'

Ali looked closely as she could at the face of the jaguar. He almost looked accepting of his faith and slipped away like sand through fingers and just like he was gone.

The Peruvian fighter looked exhausted, his head hanging, he knew the fight was over too, Yuki sighed, 'He called his affinity animal too early, they are the most energy-draining move possible.'

Yuki's teaching of the sport included an in-depth history of how affinity animals came about. It takes years of practice and the study of the animal you want to recreate.

The Malaysian fighter rose her hands from her sides and once again flames jump to life in her arms and she hurled fireball after fireball across the arena. The Peruvian shields deflect them away but the fire kept coming closer and closer. The Peruvian stood still, arms by his side, trusting his friends to keep him from harm but his head followed the fire. One ball was passing a boundary that none have passed before. The right shield decided not to deflect but to change the energy to water which he pushed carelessly away, some of the water landed on their fighter who cried out in pain, the water that was flames moment ago, scorched the fighter who was now kneeling, head buried in his knees. The crowd gasped and some jump to their feet.

'Will they stop the fight now?' Ali asked, worried for the burned dueller.

'No, it is up to them to surrender but this kind of thing happens all the time. Sometimes it's easier to change energy than to manipulate but it can still retain some of its properties like heat,' Yuki explained.

The speed at which the fire was bombarding the Peruvians was relentless. The Peruvian shields were tiring and they moved closer to their fighter to use less energy and that's when the fire coming at them picked up speed again. The shields moved to stand in front of their fighter and together created a small bubble force field that surrounded the three of them.

The fire continued to rain down and soon surrounded them in a tornado, through the leaping gaps in the fire, cracks started to appear in the force field. Suddenly, the force field collapsed and the fire went out. The Malaysian fighter lowers her hands and nodded at the Peruvian team, who returned the nod. Formal bowing which signed the end of the match started, the whole team bowed to each other, then left shields bowed to each other first then the fighters, then the right shields, the final bow was one as the whole team once again bowed to each other.

The two teams crossed the space between to shake hands, then the Peruvian team walked quickly as they could out of the arena where a man wearing healer robes waited for them at the exit. The crowd clapped for both teams and a cheer went up when the Malaysian team made a small bow to the crowd.

Yuki leaned back in her seat, petting Rex's head and gives him a scratch behind the ear which at this point his tail started to wag. 'Well, that team did not study, the Malaysian teams are famous for their fire-wielding. That match was very short. I think we should stay and watch another one, what do you think?' Yuki said, smiling at Ali.

Ali grinned back, 'I don't see the harm.'

Reece Yuki shouted over to him, 'Reece, can we stay for another match?'

Reece, who seemed to have procured some kind of food that looked and smelled equally temping garbled in between bites, 'Don't worry, I don't plan on going anywhere until the team I placed a bet on wins.'

'Reece, that's bad luck and I don't think we are meant to do that kind of thing,' Yuki said, turning to Ali for help.

'You can't undo a bet,' Ali smiled more to herself as she was the one Reece had asked for bet advice but all she could supply was to watch out for the team duel record, which was the knowledge she picked up from Yuki's extensive teaching of the subject.

Luckily for their jobs of patrolling, the team that Reece placed the bet came out next the match was fast-paced with short attacks that had the crowd gasping and Yuki on the edge of her seat, it was over in half an hour with Reece's team losing and Yuki shouting, 'I told you!' repeatedly.

As they left the arena, Ali and Yuki walked together and Yuki recounted the history of the arena and how it was the home of the longest match to ever take place in the history of battling.

'Eight hours long, can you imagine it? Fighters and shields collapsed from exhaustion.' Yuki rushed painting a battle scene picture. But Ali couldn't imagine fighting for that long, though she had no doubt that teams like those became the heroes of schoolyards and people who followed the sport as passionately as Yuki did.

Chapter 5
Mist Down

A man with a small child in tow approached them and declared himself and his son lost. Yuki started to cough and Ali knew that she wouldn't confess that they were lost too so she pulled out her map on which nothing was marked out. 'We will find the place together,' she smiled, hoping she sounded more confident than she felt.

The man's name was Lorenzo and his son was Sid. They had gone to a find a bathroom but on the way back so many more tents had been put up so they had no idea where they were their tent was.

'Do you remember what kind of area your tent was in?' Ali queried.

'It is the craft section but it turns out there are five different craft sections close together and each has hundreds of tents in them. It is our first year here,' Lorenzo confessed.

Ali was beginning to question her navigation skills. 'I am sure we will find it soon enough,' she smiled at them and started to walk she hoped was the right way.

'So what do you sell or display?' Yuki asked Lorenzo.

'Painting mostly, I am from the Valley of Spoken Stones, have you heard of it?'

'Yes, but my history is a bit shaky. A Stone Skin priestess found a magic valley. Is it the rocks of the valley that can speak of the people born there or the valley can hear the rocks,' Ali guessed. She made a mental note to start reading in her spare time again, not that she had much of that.

'No one really knows, a lot of people say both but touching a stone tells me how old it is or I can hear the heart sound or the song of its birth, which regularly sound like mountains crushing each other but every so often, stones will give up an image like their fiery birth or when they were laying on the bottom of the sea or a river bed and that's what I paint, well, I did until we got lost,' Lorenzo smiled and shrugged his shoulders and turn to his son. 'Are you doing alright?'

'Yes, can I go over to that stall there?' They followed the pointing finger to a stall that was surrounded with children. Lorenzo nodded and Sid ran straight for the stall. Ali thought Sid looked like he was enjoying being lost, which was a good thing because lost was what they were going to be for a while.

'That's amazing,' Ali said astonished, the geography very much appealing to her.

'Ya, it's my life but talking to stones does not pay well, unfortunately, but we are happy,' he said, smiling at his son, who seemed to have made new friends.

They did not get far when they stumbled upon another team and Ali decided that she needed a second opinion on her chosen direction.

The navigation head of the other team named Will admitted, he too was having a hard time trying to read the map but he was sure he had seen gallery quarter not far. 'Some of the tents that aren't stationary have moved around so the map is not one hundred percent,' Will explained. 'Some people don't like their plot wanting shade or the sun or reasons so the tents can dance around.'

'I will just check in with my Cap to see if I can take you there myself,' Will offered and he walked away to stick his head in a tent. He returned grinning behind him as tent flaps moved to revile a very familiar captain.

'Hello Kara,' grinned Ali.

'I knew we meet so but I did not suspect this soon, how are you today Jenks?' asked Kara, hands on hips.

'Better, thank you.' Jenks nodded.

'Where is Philip?' Kara asked, looking around, scanning the market area behind them.

'We don't know, we were just asked to keep a presence and move up the mountain later,' Reece conveyed.

Ali confess the story of their day so far and it felt good to tell someone in the know about being lost and not much help to anyone.

'Will, could you please escort Lorenzo and Sid to their stall?' instructed Kara. 'I have a job for this team.'

They said their goodbyes and apologies to Lorenzo and Sid but Lorenzo waved the apology away and said, 'It is better to be lost together sometimes, you should come around to my stall some time if you can find it,' he chuckled lightly.

Ali still felt pretty useless and she hoped the next task set to them would go better.

'There are fights we have to break up. There are usually fights and little scraps every year, lots of people, lots of alcohol, it happens. This year the fest counsel has called for some job swapping among teams that have worked at the festival for years, this could be a good or bad idea, I don't know, but all that matters is we do our job right. We carry the pride of Atlantis and the history of this Fest on our backs. It will be tougher this year with all the anti-human riots taking place this year.' Kara looked everyone in the face then nodded and walked back into her tent. 'Once you put on that uniform, you stand for something, Yuki and Ali, Phillip told me you were going to graduate soon and thought you two could do with some extra experience,' she smiled.

'Oh, thanks for thinking of us,' Yuki laughed, but Ali knew that laugh was fake and she was nervous.

Kara seemed to understand, said, 'No one has ever got seriously injured before last year before,' and she pushed through the red and purple fabric to enter her tent.

Ali felt as if she were going to walk into a war, crowd control no longer sounded easy beside her, Yuki petted Rex. 'I have never been in a fight before,' she whispered.

Ali was not sure how she was going to reassure Yuki when she was never been in a fight either but she could not bring herself to tell reassuring lies. Their first fight was going before graduation. They had never been the opposition before. On their last mission, they were just fire fighters. The Fire Martins weren't throwing fire at them. She didn't think training counted even though they had both received years of hand-to-hand and magic fighting, they always knew they were there to learn and no one was severely harmed besides bruises.

'Though, I think my brothers would be proud, can't wait to tell them about it,' Yuki tried .

Thank the gods at least one of us is starting to think positively about this, thought Ali to herself. Kara walked out of her tent with a small shield on her back, a gun and a short sword strapped to her hips. Ali noted with small relief that her face was not the only one to fall.

Ali thought Kara herself now looked nervous but she was doing her best to hide it and said, 'It's just for show, just tell that we are more ready for this fight than they are.'

'Should we wait for Will?' asked Kara's team Med.

'No, he knows where to go,' she said and gave Ali a pointed look before winking at her.

There were eight of them, Ali thought, Kara's team were missing, Will and Reece's team missing their captain. Phil would have been a good person in this kind of situation. He would just shout and people tell them they were idiots and to go home or he would reason with them and make them see common sense but they all usually listened to him.

They started to walk, Jenks talked to the other med whose name was Erik about what sounded like supplies. Yuki introduced herself and Rex to the other sense whose sign was a small dog.

'I thought you were a fire ward, how came the job change?' said Ali.

'I was one of the head fire wards for this fest for the last 10 years. I was good at my job to know I was but I think it's some kind of promotion as well the council wanting to mix things up,' said Kara.

'So how is Phil doing?' Kara asked Reece and Ali.

'We saw him this morning but that was all he did not say much either,' replied Reece.

'It's hard losing someone and no one can really console you, you just find a way to live with it though you might get a little lost on the way,' said Kara.

'It's only right to get lost to find something you lost,' said Ali.

Kara and Reece nodded and they walked in silence for a while. It was late in the afternoon when they came to the edge of the tents. They walked around the back of the tents to find a large clearing surrounded by trees. There were a few people standing around who did not look pleased to see them Ali though.

Shouting came from the tent at the side of the clearing. They retreated to the centre of the clearing, away from the noise. The tents began to shake as if they were coming to life and the noise increased. Suddenly, people burst forth from the tents, pushing and shoving each other. People kept pouring out of the tents and they were soon surrounded by the angry mob that moment ago wanted nothing then to tear each other apart. *Now we had given them an enemy to share*, thought Ali. We are the enemy, she inhaled, readying herself to use her power.

'Looks like we are just on time this year,' said Kara. 'Yuki, Ali, how about we give them a frosty welcome?'

Yuki inhaled, putting out her hand in front of her, the air temperature dropped to freezing and the grass they stood on to the grass at the feet of the crowd turned sliver. Yuki nodded to Ali, who raised a howling wind to whip around them for a moment or two before letting it die. She could feel some people in the crowd pulling power to themselves but no one moved.

There were only eight of them but they had the law on their side and Ali hoped that counted for something here.

'Return to the festival and please refrain from fighting or I will have you all arrested,' shouted Kara some people turned away and disappeared, the warning was enough for them but Ali was sure they would not be able to carry out the warning if the fight did come to pass.

Her mind went back to combat training classes with Yuki and she had missed or skipped a couple of the classes over the years for various reasons. None of the reasons like a longer break seemed like good reasons now. There was no way she was going to be able to bury the guilt now and she hoped they did not miss anything important.

A ball of fire came out of the crowd and straight towards them, Kara stopped the ball in mid-flight, extinguished it with a click of her fingers. Ali threw up a force field but there was no need for it and she let it drop but stayed ready.

'Alright you are all under arrest for the attempted harming of festival security and Atlantis guardians,' Kara shouted and stepped forward, no one moved again, not quite shouting this time.

'Erik, I want them all,' Kara said.

Erik stepped forward to stand beside Kara, electricity sparking and crackling from his hands. Yuki let the temperature plummet further so everyone breathed out white clouds. Ali was waiting for a signal from Kara so she could create a wall of air to hold them in place.

'Now!' shouted Kara, the crowd broke and ran away from them, Erik let blots of energy fly into the crowd but they hit no one. 'Ali, will you help them run along?' asked Kara. Ali nodded, putting a strong gust of wind at theirs backs to push them in the right direction.

They were soon standing in the clearing all alone, Ali let the wind flight for a little bit longer just to tell the crowd that their presence remained there.

'I think it's time to take a break much deserved after no bloodshed and no one to arrest,' said Kara.

'What about the one who threw the fire?' exclaimed Reece.

'Don't worry, I will tell the other fire warrants to keep an eye out for them. Every fire is different. It can be read like a signature. They are on their last chance,' Kara insured.

'True, every fire is different to us Fire Nixes,' agreed Jenks.

The team found a tree to sit under and Jenks had wisely packed food, which they devoured. 'Why this year?' asked Jenks, 'why the change in teams?'

'People fight it happens all the time and it's natural but this mass fight, it's an organised affair and people got really hurt last year and someone nearly died. Of course, we never found out who was behind it but a source from high up in the chain of things told me that some teams were turning a blind to fights so that's why there is a change this year,' said Kara who was shaking food crumbs from her clothes.

They chatted for and while and Yuki practised creating her affinity animal 'Look, Rex! It's you,' Yuki said, pointing to the small dog made of ice, Rex sniffed at the air but did not look very impressed.

'I thought you were going to start practising over different elements?' said Ali.

Yuki sighed, 'I know. I just thought I would work on how the dog moved some more.' The dog moved slowly along a small sheet of ice Yuki had made for it.

Ali knew that it was harder to create a creature over an element that was not your own. There were four different types of battle areas: stone, sand, water, and ice. Yuki had recreated Rex over stone once but she could not hold the shape for very long.

Yuki let the ice dog melt and turned to Ali. 'Celeb can create ice dragon over any element he wants,' Yuki sighed again.

'Yuki, your brothers have been battling for years now. You should just give yourself a little bit of time,' encouraged Ali.

'Ah, you have never tried hard to make an affinity?' challenged Yuki.

'Come on, Yuki, you know what it's like for me. The air never wants to sit still that's why you don't see any Sylph fighter with affinity creators. Don't you remember the window I broke in that base a couple of months ago trying to make you a cat or something?'

'Oh, I remember,' Yuki laughed, 'that thing like nothing like a cat.'

They carried out patrols with Kara's team for the rest of the day. Relaxed, they stroll at an easy pace, enjoying music and the cooling sun. They stopped at a stall dedicated to desserts. Tempting at a distance and mouth-watering up close, Ali brought a mini coconut and cherry tart. Ali remembered inhaling the divine smell trying to savour it because it was gone in three mouthfuls. The team treated themselves to various gifts and souvenirs. Ali purchased a volcano pin and a postcard picturing tents with Xerhina and Okowazira in the background to send home. They also stopped at a Fire Martian's stall selling beautiful glass jewellery encasing flickering flames. 'Charming and useful if you are a Fire Martin like me,' the stall explained. He picked up a bead and clicked his finger of his other hand as the flame appeared and was gone from the bead. He placed the demonstration beam into a bowl with clear beads. While the glass there is special, it is only the flame jars that allow us to take a portion. Reece and Jenks brought pendants and Reece brought a bead bracelet, the orange glow showing up more as the evening settled around them. There were no more incidents but they kept a keen eye out when they were being tempted by more food. They gave into curiosity a few more times until it was time to head up the mountain for the closing ceremony.

They reached the mountaintop before midnight to find the caldera with a lake at its heart ringed by crowds. Ali was surprised by how well she could see everything, with only a few fires and a full moon to light the landscape. There was an eerie silence that did not seem right to Ali. With this many people around, they just looked to the dark blue lake for their answers.

A quiet chant began to fill the bowl of the mountaintop, a sibilance, like someone was whispering right into her ear, a shiver went down her spine because no one was standing near her, and neither could she tell which direction it was coming from.

Everyone moved away from the lakeshore to higher ground. A mist had started to form in the middle of the caldera spread outwards, engulfing the whole lake. In places, the crowd parted to let monks in long blue hooded robes through and down to the lake, though none passed close to her. She knew they were the source of the chant.

The people in robes disappeared into the mist, Ali moved over to Jenks. 'What's happening?' she whispered.

'Those in the blue robes will drink from the lake and will be able to see the fortunes of people in the mist. They become oracles for the night, everyone must standalone for this part, as only can they know their future,' said Jenks.

Ali nodded and retreated back to her place quietly to stand and watch. As the night wore on, Ali saw the oracles approach people with advice or a piece of their future. Some people left without the words of an oracle. Either they saw what they needed to see in the mist themselves or they knew enough time had passed waiting and the oracles did not have anything to say to them.

Something in Ali's mind compelled her to look towards and into the mist but she could see nothing, then right where she was looking in the wall of mist, a cloaked figure emerged and walked straight towards her. It was like a nightmare, thinking about the evil always made it appear.

Ali did not want this person to come any closer, she did not expect the oracles to talk to her and all of a sudden, she did not want to hear from their lips but she knew she had to let them say their words.

A man with a patchy beard stopped right in front of her, he seemed to be ageless and as if he had always lived in the mist he did not meet her eyes and looked all around as if searching for someone else then he finally brought his eyes to meet Ali's.

'It is you,' he said, nodding.

Ali did not know what so she nodded back.

They stared at each other for a while, the man breathed in deeply once. 'Time is running out, the clock is going back,' the man walked away.

Ali felt dread at those words and she had no idea why, and that's when she noticed an oracle talking to Yuki. A chant rose from within the mist, it had a different rhythm to the last and Ali knew the ceremony was finished. She knew the monks could see no more than glimpses of maybe futures. Any longer in the mist and the monk would become lost but Ali felt a little lost at their words.

The team was the last to leave, making sure everyone who attended made it safely back down the mountain. They said their goodnights to Kara and her team, as well as other guardians. As walked back to the ship, Ali told Yuki what the oracle said. 'I know don't why but that sounds bad, Ali,' said Yuki.

'The oracle told me that I must return home.'

Chapter 6
The Need for Truth

Ali sat upfront with Reece in the glass cockpit, they were flying over open water now, enormous white-capped waves crashing below them. Ali thought the water looked cold. They had passed the island from which the recovery mission was being launched but gave the island a wide birth. Phil did not want them to be seen and they continued far out into the ocean. Ali planned a route that avoided the main ship routes and sea channels. Their avoidance route still could be intersected by airships at overlaps so they flew low that these points. Captain Philip then covered the messaging orb to block out incoming messages plus, just in case someone from the Volt was monitoring their ship. Ali worked out a distance of radar ranges from the common ship but she had no codes for Shadow ships.

'Hey, do guys remember when Yuki and Ali broke the messaging orb when they tried to call friends on another ship?' Reece laughed.

Ali cringed at Reece, trying to lighten the mood at their expense, they had just paid the cost from their wages last month.

'What did the other captain say when she picked up…oh ya! Not taking personal call ladies, and you two dropped it,' chuckled Reece.

'Maybe not the time Reece,' Jenks whispered, then standing to nudge Reece with an elbow.

Ali turned to gauge the captain's reaction but Yuki pointed to a dent in the metal floor like Ali needed reminding. The spot where the orb filled with both their magic fell from the mezzanine, exploding on impact.

'I broke a few when I was training,' Captain Philip admitted ruefully.

Ali's jaw dropped, well he certainly did say anything about that when they dropped that orb nope, he was as mad as the last king but fairer.

'Who were you calling?' Yuki asked.

'More than a friend,' Captain Philip coughed.

There were a few giggles before they all fell silent, Ali thought they would all break rules to talk to a friend, now they were breaking rules to see a brother.

Ali thought that without saying anything to each other, the team had agreed that their captain had a right to be there when they brought up this brother's ship. Though the captain did try and ditch them that morning, Reece made the point that the captain needed them and well, we needed him to stick around, to continue being their captain.

'We are two miles out from their location,' shouted Reece.

'Alright, Reece, take us in slowly,' ordered the captain, who was coming down the stairs from his office. He walked over to stand by Reece and looked out the window to watch other ships moving about point up ahead. He did take his eyes from the window. 'What we are doing will most likely have consequences for all of us and some of you have not even graduated yet but thank you,' Phil spoke sombrely, everyone remained silent.

Ali leaned closer to the window, squinting to see what was happening. She could make out two massive ships in the water and six ships flying in circles above them. The two sea ships were parallel with a wide space of water between, almost as if they were lining up to exchange shots. Ali couldn't believe her eyes. It was the Erebus and the Veracity, the stars and pride of Atlantis, their largest warships, she had only ever seen photos. Jenks and Yuki had their faces plaster to the window too. 'We are dead,' muttered Jenks Ali agreed there was no getting away now.

A crackling voice came in over the radio. 'This zone is off-limits to all unauthorised ships. State your name and propose,' the voice ordered.

'This is Captain Philip of the Redfish,' said Phil, leaning over Reece to talk into the radio.

'State your propose,' the voice barked.

'I am here to see my brother Captain Ray of the Two Tails ship,' Phil retorted.

A different voice broke over the radio. 'Captain Philip, you are ordered to land on the Erebus now,' spoke the grave voice. The Erebus was the larger of the two ships completely grey while the Veracity was striped grey and black.

They circled the ship once before landing on the completely empty land deck. 'All team members are required to disembark your ship, Captain,' called the first voice over the radio.

Phil turned to face his crew. 'Don't speak until I do,' he ordered and walked towards the door. Ali nodded with the rest of them and followed him. *I mean what I am to say to them. Hi, I am part of an illegal flight, misused ship codes and lanes*, Ali thought grimly. They knew all this now.

They stepped out onto the deck and Ali could not get over the size of the Erebus, there was room for twenty ships to land with room to spare. A group of people descended stairs that belonged to the highest of the three towers on the ship. Once that the bottom of the stairs they took formation around one man and a woman flanking them on two sides. *He must be the head of the operation, judging by his uniform and a high councillor by her robes to act as a witness,* thought Ali.

Ali knew Atlantis had sea ships but had never imaged anything this big, let alone to see it with her own eyes and then to stand on its deck as she looked around more, she began to see a symbol she had seen only very few times before, it was the emblem of the Shadow Guardians. A simple ringed Atlantis which they all wore but here a giant bird hung over Atlantis and a whale in the water below it which was the sign of the secret branch of guardians. These were shadow guardians but their education did not go any further in details other than shadows will always outrank guardians, even a low shadow out ranked general captain guardians. Their role was to keep the veil between the worlds, working with the curse, among other undisclosed tasks. Magic and people did not abide by the curse. The effects or consequences of magic can spill into the human world and humans unknowingly to them in encroach on the magic world.

'Captain Philip,' called the man at the centre of the group, 'I am Captain Marcus and this is Councillor Esmeralda, you were warned by the high council not to come here and now I will have to escort you and your team back to Atlantis.'

'I have a right to be here,' called Philip.

'Captain Philip, I am sorry for your loss but I have orders to carry out and you had an order directly from Lunglock to stay away!' exasperated Marcus.

'He was my brother!' shouted Phil.

Captain Marcus looked away for a few minutes before he exhaled slowly. 'Others had lost too.'

'You and your team will be escorted to the observation tower. There you will remain until we return to Atlantis also no evidence will be touched by you before our return. Is that understood?' Marcus pressed.

It was Phil's turn to look away. He agreed with the Shadow Captain. 'We will do as you say,' he promised.

A man from one of the towers came running up to their group. 'The pilots are asking for permission and Captain Artemis is calling from the Veracity,' he huffed out of breath.

'Granted,' Marcus barked and the man ran back.

'What are they going to do?' asked Phil.

Marcus turned to face the airship. 'They will drop searching chains,' he exclaimed.

Ali turned to see four of them flying ships from a square low over the water. Doors on the underbelly of the ships opened and out fell one swirling metal sphere from each ship. The ship doors closed and all four ascended to land on the Veracity opposite them.

'Captain Philip, can you get your pilot to remove your ship from the middle of my deck?' Marcus ordered, marching back to the tower. *He seemed as tense as they all felt*, Ali thought.

Reece looked sheepish as Philip turned to Reece. 'Do as he says and put it in the far corner over there,' spoke Philip quietly.

'I'll go with him,' said Ali and the two walked back to the Redfish. Behind them, Ali heard Marcus say to some guards, 'You stay with them and bring them back to the tower. The rest of you follow me.'

Reece mumbled, 'Thanks, Ali.' As one of Marcus's men caught up with them.

They were walking back from the newly parked ship and Ali watched four chains rise out of the water, two of the larger airships worked opposite each other. They lower themselves and collected two chains each. The airships rose higher and the chains grew longer but there was no sign of what they were pulling up from below.

They had reached the middle of the deck again when the water at the ends of the chains began to boil and froth. A mangled airship wrapped in chains emerged out of the water. The broken ship was only inches above the water, Ali could see the Veracity opposite them was sending out more chains from its hull to form a net beneath. Bang! A shot exploded from the broken ship and fired upon one of the pulling ships.

Ali stopped walking, shocked into stillness. The pulling ship tried to jerk up away from the fire to but the chains still tendered it, holding it fast. The ship fell to the side, the fire blowing off the whole right wing of the ship. Chains snapped and the ship with one wing was thrown high from the force of the releasing tension. The other pulling ship was hit by the loose chains which cleaved off the back end. The ship, now still tied to the broken ship, started to fall into the water.

Ali screamed and with her mind reached for the pulling ship that was going to hit the water first. She ripped apart the binding chains and the broken ship fell into the hull net. She lifted up the airship with no tail, dropping it on the deck of the Veracity. Ali searched the skies for the other pulling ship. It was far and falling fast, too far, panicked Ali, running to the edge of the deck. Arms outstretched, she dragged the ship to her. She did not know why the ship was no longer on fire, whether she did that or maybe someone onboard did. She had the ship follow her hands, bringing right over her head and landing it on the deck near her.

Ali was aware of the panic and action rising all around her, all over the sea ship people ran to their stations and people ran to recuse those on board the half charred airship.

Ali also noticed that she was standing on the very edge of the deck but she did not care because she was very tired now. Closing her eyes, she fell into the water.

Chapter 7
The Ruling

Ali first noticed the pain before she opened her eyes, a pain that seeped out of her bones flooding her body. She did not want to open her eyes but someone called out her name, 'Ali, Ali please wake up this time!' the voice implored.

Ali opened her eyes, she was in a small bed with a white metal ceiling above her, more metal beams running through it, she turned her head in the direction the voice had come from.

To find Yuki sitting in a chair beside her bed. 'Yuki' she croaked, Yuki closed the book she had been reading with a bang.

'Oh, Ali, finally you're awake. Rex and I thought you were going to sleep the whole way back to Atlantis,' Yuki exclaimed.

Rex pushed his head into her arm. Ali tried to lift herself but found she could not without pain.

'What happened?' She looked back at Yuki.

'You don't remember? Well, you saved a lot of people and then you collapsed, you fell thirty feet off the ship into the water.'

Ali tried to sit up but cried out, falling back into the bed. 'The doctors said you would be in a lot of pain, will I go and get one,' Yuki asked halfway out of her chair now.

'No, it's alright. Can you help me?' said Ali.

Yuki helped Ali to sit and piled a load of pillows behind her back. Ali sighed. She felt disorientated, vague memories flitted through her mind.

'Yuki, can you tell me everything? I feel out of the loop,' Ali pleaded.

'Well, Reece tried to jump in after you but a bunch of men stopped him and they sent a team to get you. It was high Councillor Esmeralda who saved you, she a mermaid I didn't know, did you? Then you have been asleep for nearly two days,' Yuki blurted in a rush. 'You have had a couple of visitors, mainly our team, doctors and Captain Marcus and the Councillor,' Yuki expanded.

'Wow, this is something not to write home about,' Ali joked, her mind coming back to the present. 'How is Philip? What's going to happen when we get back to Atlantis?'

'The best we could hope for Philip is no longer going to be charged but he is going to lose the Redfish and his job until the investigation is over, just a suspension,' Yuki said correcting herself quickly with a shrug then coming in closer. 'There is something else. There was another person on board the Two Tails.'

'Who was it?'

'They don't know the nav, med, pilot, sense and Ray have all been identified.'

'What is going to happen to our team?' asked Ali, hoping for some good news.

'Captain Marcus seems to have an answer for that, he said he is always looking for people like you and I told him that you don't go anywhere without us,' Yuki chipped, clearly excited. 'Plus there has been talk of you taking the magic level test again.'

'I don't know if I want to join the secret guardians, I like the work we do now. It's simple and we are allowed to talk to people about our missions. I don't think the secret guardians can talk about their work at all,' said Ali. 'As for the magic test, I don't think I have gone up a level just a fluke.'

'Ah, but you have to admit, it would be a lot more interesting. We would be flying modern ships and working in advanced teams, which I learned today just means nearly double the numbers of an ordinary team but the people in them tend to be very powerful,' Yuki admitted.

'Well, maybe it's not a bad idea to join for a little while, Reece could have a co-pilot,' said Ali.

'I think they might be making him the co-pilot,' laughed Yuki.

Ali laughed too and wished she hadn't, 'Yuki, do think I could get anything for the pain and maybe some food. I am really hungry all of a sudden.'

'Sure, I better tell one of the doctors you're awake anyway now,' Yuki confessed and she left with Rex swanning out the door behind her.

Yuki soon returned with not one but three doctors in tow.

After poking and prodding, they declared that she was well enough to eat and handed over some medicine for her pain. With that over, Yuki brought a small feast for the both of them to Ali's bedside. Ali surprised herself and Yuki by how much she ate but when the doctors returned later to check on her, it was normal because she had spent a lot of energy using her powers but were a little surprised themselves when they learned Ali could have probably eaten more.

The doctors left muttering to one another. 'The rest of the team should be dropping by soon,' said Yuki. 'They went to support Philip in his meeting with the other ship officers.'

'Did they find anything out about the broken ship?' Ali pressed her mind to return to the Two Tails, not that it left her mind, really.

'No just the bodies' said Yuki, looking at the floor. 'The Councillor said a blessing over them, she also asked about you but was too busy to come herself.' Ali how have to meet her properly to thank her soon she though equal amounts nervous and grateful.

'How far away are we from Atlantis?' asked Ali.

'Three days,' said Jenks, walking into the room with Phillip and Reece. 'Even though we are the fastest ship in the Atlantis fleet.'

'Not fast enough,' growled Phillip, 'How are you feeling today Ali?'

All glances landed on her, 'Well, everything hurts and I am a bit tired but other than that I am alright.' Ali tried to sit up more in the bed.

'Ya well, you did drop like a stone.' Reece joked.

'Thank you, Reece,' Ali mocked.

'We are very proud of you Ali and you should be proud of yourself too for want you did,' said Phillip and the others nodded in agreement with him.

Ali knew that they all cared about her and she loved the family they had become, it made her feel better having them around but the tiredness remained so when her eyelids began to droop, Phillip decided it was time to leave her to get some sleep.

Ali couldn't remember the door closing behind them but then she didn't remember falling asleep either.

*

When Ali woke, she presumed a new day had started but she was not sure as there was no window in the room, she realised and that bothered her. Getting up, she found a clean set of her own robes folded neatly in a locker beside the bed.

She stepped outside her room and the thought came to her that she had no idea where she was on the ship. She decided that she should only take stairs going up and that should bring her out onto the deck for some fresh air at some point.

She passed very few people on her ascend and those who she meets just stared at her. Somehow the ship began an eerie place to be wondering about by one's self. Countless stairs later, Ali saw the sky through a door window. She ran for the door and burst out through it. Breathing hard now, she stood on deck finally, she looked for a place to sit down that would be out of people's way and sight. The base of a tower provided for her needs of shade and back support. She watched the waves appear and disappear, it felt good to feel the sea breeze on her skin. She watched the Veracity moving alongside them with two broken ships on the deck.

Ali looked back to the Erebus's deck here was a ship with one wing, she only vaguely remembered putting it there. A team moved about it, assessing the damage, she wondered whether they would repair it or recycle it. The shade over her darkened, Ali jumped. She couldn't believe Yuki had got so close without her realising.

'I am sorry, did I scare you?' Yuki apologised but her smile said she had planned to all along.

'No.' Ali lied and Yuki slid down the wall, landing with a bump beside her. She threw one leg over the other, then Rex lay his head across them.

'There are some people who would like to meet you if you are up for it?' asked Yuki.

'Soon, where are they?' she asked.

Yuki nodded across to the ship with one wing. 'It's just a couple of crew members,' said Yuki.

'Did they find out as to why Captain Ray's ship fired upon them?'

'There are two possibilities, the first is that they were fighting someone before they went down and we activated the fighting system when we pulled the ship up. The second reason is not much better, the ship could have been set with a trap so whoever tried to interfere with it would be fired upon,' said Yuki, letting out a breath.

Ali did not like mystery stories, *they did not have any answers, just more questions*, Ali thought, letting out a sigh of frustration.

'So, should we meet these people then?' Ali suggested changing the subject. Standing up proofed difficult as the sea became rougher and the great ship swayed under them. Rex looked the most sable of them both and he walked off without them.

'Traitor,' growled Yuki after him.

They across the deck with a little stagger here and a little stagger there. Ali was still too tired to draw on her powers.

A man approached them. 'Hello, is your captain here?' asked Ali.

'I am Darshan, the pilot,' he said, shaking Ali's hand. 'Thanks for saving us back there, I will get him for you now.' A man who stuck his head in a door shouted something Ali couldn't understand. Darshan left, walking around the back of the airship, disappearing.

'By the drown king,' Yuki pulled at Ali's arm. 'That was Darshan!'

'Who?'

'A champion duel fighter,' Yuki grinned.

'Ah, hello,' said a young man, stepping out from behind a different door. 'It's the women who destroyed the entire undercarriage of my ship when she dropped it on deck.' His face conveyed no emotion.

Ali felt angry and would have given him a piece of her mind if she was not so tired and if Yuki had not got there before her.

'She saved you and all of your crew plus she can put your ship at the bottom of the ocean if you don't like it here,' explained Yuki in a calm voice. Ali knew she was definitely not able to but it was nice to think Yuki believed she could.

The man suddenly smiled broadly. 'No doubt she could,' he said, looking to Ali, 'thank you for recusing us but you still destroyed my ship.'

'You were missing a whole a wing before I decided to recuse you,' said Ali

'Wings are easy to replace,' the man shrugged.

'Kye,' shouted a man in captain robes walking from around the back of the ship 'Why is this ship still not ready? I needed this ship up and running yesterday.'

Kye turned to face his captain, 'I am afraid that's not possible. We will have to go Atlantis for more parts if not a whole new ship if you wanted it back that fast. I am still finding problems in here.'

'Alright, call Atlantis and see what they got,' relented the captain.

Kye nodded to Yuki and her then climbed back into the ship.

'Good afternoon, I am Captain Alexander, I see you met Kye, my mechanic. He is a bit ship proud, I heard you are going to be down a captain on your team so you are very welcome to join mine.'

'We still have to graduate before we can even think of joining another team,' Ali interjected.

'Oh yes, of course, I forgot, maybe I will see you both after you graduate then,' said Captain Alexander.

'Maybe,' said Ali, smiling politely as she could. *There was no way they were going to abandon their captain now*, she thought.

'Well, it was lovely to meet you both but I am a very busy man and must be on my way,' mused Alexander and he left.

'He didn't even say thank you,' Yuki grumbled, throwing an arm in his direction of departure.

'I know but that doesn't bother me,' Ali said, 'let's just get out of here. I think that man wouldn't mind if our team split up.'

'I know just the place,' said Yuki, 'this ship has a massive library which I borrowed a book from yesterday.'

'Let me guess, you can't find the library now,' said Ali.

'Yes, that is true but what is a better excuse for spooning around the ship than being lost.'

Chapter 8
Booked

The sliver towers of Atlantis shone on the horizon, Yuki and Ali never did find the library by the time the ships pulled into the harbour.

The team packed up everything they owed from the Redfish. They could pack the rest of their stuff from the student dorm island after graduation. *It could be their last time together as a team*, Ali thought gloomily. 'I hope this is not the last time I see our ship,' Ali admitted, looking around the Redfish, feeling nostalgia.

'She will be flying again very soon,' called Reece from the front of the ship. He was checking switches and mumbling about colours. 'Hey Yuki, is that gage reading red or orange to you,' asked Reece.

'That's definitely red, Reece. What is that for anyway,' Yuki asked.

'Can't help if I am colour blind, landing I think,' exclaimed Reece squinting at the control closer.

'Yuki, Ali,' Jenks shouted from outside the ship 'Captain Marcus is here to talk to you.'

Ali stood up from her bunk where she had been folding some clothes, hitting her head on the bunk above. 'I'll be out in a minute,' she yelled back, clutching her head, trying to hold back curses. 'I always speak too soon don't need to see the ship for a while now,' she sighed.

Ali stepped outside, with Yuki and Rex following.

'Good morning,' called Captain Marcus, who was standing on the deck with Phillip. 'The ship will be staying in Atlantis for a few days. I hope you are not leaving Atlantis for too long, there will be an inquiry about what happened with the recovered wreck.' Turning his cool gaze on Ali. 'All going well after you both graduate, you are welcome to come back, a place on my team is sought after position. I trust you know where my office is?' he tried to smile but Ali thought maybe he did not know how.

'I am sure we will find it,' assured Ali, *Gods! You get lost once and everyone knows*, thought Ali.

'Oh, this yours,' Yuki said brightly, handing her library book to Marcus.

'So it is,' accepted Marcus. 'Thank you. I will be seeing you all soon, I think.' He gave a nod to Phillip and left.

'Is everything alright, Captain?' Asked Ali.

'Yes, just needed permission to fly the Redfish to the hanger at Atlantis's main base, come on inside. I need to have a quick talk with you all.' Corralled Phillip.

Once they were all sitting together on the Redfish in a messy circle, Phillip cleared his throat, 'I just want to thank you all, I know I have not been a good captain as of late, putting you in danger and in trouble with the law.'

'We would do it all again with you, Sir,' interjected Jenks, Ali agreed with him nodding along with the team.

'I know.' He took a breath. 'Our team is going to be broken up but I just want you to be careful about where and who you join up with. If you choose to join the secret guardians, there are laws that bind you to their secrets and they are very hard to get away from, you may not be able to stay together, I heard two of you met a Captain Alexander the other day,' said Phillip.

'Yes Ali and I met him, he said we are welcome to join his team,' Yuki confessed.

'Captain Alexander is the worst of them. I know you are meant to go out into the world and make up your own opinions on people and things but please be wary of the Shadows, it is not something you sign up for they chose you. He is proud of his team for all the wrong reasons. Every member is a powerhouse in their own right. He is kind of a collector, you could say. On his team, there are six people who used to be the world champions in duelling a team of triples and a team from Greenland. These people are trained in the fighting and were some of the best at it and they just left the world stage to join his team.'

'I remember those teams, the Lucast triplets, Shamor, Ralfa, Marwex and we meet Darshan the other day,' Yuki piped in. 'Both of those teams dropped out of the championships a couple of years ago and no one knew why.'

'Well, Alexander is probably the main reason. There is another man called Kye on his team and rumour says that the Atlantis high council wanted him for the High Guard. I don't know how or why but Alexander seems to gather people for the Shadows. Alexander once ran for the High Guard himself but was turned down, then he became his own captain. It said that he also ran for head of the shadow Guardians but Atlantis gave it to Marcus instead. You don't give powerful people powerful positions if you want to be able to control them. Maybe that is why he is lower rank but he has more freedom and assembled himself a very powerful crew. I don't know how you keep that kind of power in check, though. Maybe you could stay together and find a new captain. The times are strange now. It is good to have friends around.'

Ali felt sad they had become more than friends, they had become her family over the couple of seasons. She was not sure what kind of world she was stepping into anymore. It was not the clear-cut dream she had of orb trading, law, and missions. Now there were secrets, power struggles and losses, Ali thought, *maybe dreams are times when reality gets blurred because there was nothing easy about this reality.*

'We could wait until you come back,' supplied Reece.

'No, no, that might be a while, I can't ask you all to remain out of work for me.' Captain Philip straightened. 'I would say Reece and Jenks, you get yourselves straight to the Volts and see what positions are open. Yuki and Ali, they won't accept you in the Volt until after graduation. I would ask your friends to put in a word for you with their captains before the graduation job rush,' Philip offered.

'I am heading home to my family for a few days,' Captain admitted. 'Will one of you look after the scrolls?'

'Of course,' Ali nodded.

They all said their goodbyes to Captain Philip at the airship hanger. Ali knew that she would see him here again in a few days but this felt like the last time they would be together as a team. *It was hard to hear advice from the captain because it finalised the ending of their team*, Ali thought. Plus, they all had bags at their feet.

Ali walked with Yuki, Reece and Jenks to the docks, where a public airship was being unloaded of its cargo food supplies for Atlantis, no doubt for their dorms, council and the low city. Nothing grew here anymore, just the seaweed on the shores and coral below the waves. Good for the Merfolk, who had started to farm seaweed out in their new city. Nothing is ever taken from the old city below the waves. 'You're not going home, are you?' Yuki asked her.

'How did you know?' smiled Ali.

'You've got that look and the fact you didn't even try packing anything from our dorm room the last time we were there.' Yuki knew her well. Every family is messy, fighting was natural and hers was no different. Mother and Father had separated, he lived on the human side for the last couple of years. They did not see him that often because of the rocky relationship with her mother. When things between them were good, they were good but their solution to the bad times was time apart. Ali had got used to no longer bothering her. If people don't want to be bound, then nothing should bind them. Emanuel had a family of his own now, she loved them all and would make up for it soon. The pressing matter of predicting the future had to come first, time waits for no one. 'You have a good time and say hello to your family for me.' Ali hugged Yuki warmly.

'I will,' Yuki smiled back, 'but want are you going to do here?'

'I will just relax at the gym and the pool will be empty but maybe I'll sleep in. Plus, I promise to think about packing, get ready for the move from the dorms,' Ali yawned, she really hated packing.

Yuki grinned at that, they both had been looking forward to moving from student dorm living to guardian rooms, which were on different islands to the student housing. 'Alright have fun,' Yuki mocked, bending to clip a lead on Rex but he dodged her running up the gangway on the ship.

'Wow, someone is impatient,' laughed Ali.

'I know should go and see if he has stolen someone's seat,' Yuki groaned. 'I will see you in a couple of days.'

'What about you two, then?' Ali asked.

'Got to clock in some family time,' yawned Jenks, leaning back stretching. 'Plus, helping a friend move house.'

'Have fun, Jenks,' chuckled Reece, then air punching and kicking. 'I have a duel tournament in the home town.'

'Can I come and stay?' Jenks pleaded.

'The sofa is all yours,' laughed Reece, 'I just hope they don't cancel it with all anti-human riots.'

'Ah Jenks, are you sure you don't want to help me pack?' Ali implored.

'Na, I am good, besides my parent will kill me if I don't visit,' shrugged Jenks, backing up the gangway.

'Hey Jenks, maybe you open your own removals business,' laughed Reece.

'If I did, I would get to leave you behind,' grinned Jenks and hopped up the gangway. 'Bye Ali.'

'What he just say?' Reece asked mocking aghast.

Ali shrugged. 'Bye Reece.'

Ali walked to the other side of the docks to take her boat, debating on whether to eat and pack on her dorm island or to head to the Atlantis centre and hit the library. Seeing the crowds heading to the dorm, they too obviously thought of packing first, then heading home was a good idea. She saw friends and classmates among the crowd, she was tempted to join them but she had to get her worries out of the way first. Ali took the long route, it was made up of five islands and bridges from the main dock to reach the small inner islet, then on to the centre island. The only direct route from an outer island to the centre was high rock via the shadow bridge. Security precautions were in case of invasion or attack meant there would be no direct route to the centre island except from the high rock, which was a home of the shadow guardians. No attacks from Romans or Vikings because the island was hidden but from hiding, we watched as humans expanded their reach but the curse was total they still could not reach back to Atlantis even after all this time.

An hour and four bridges later, Ali walked through the arch under a watchtower on the last outer island before the bridge onto the inner islet. A reminder of a greater Atlantis. These towers were once the top of the building, weathered and repurposed, she could still see carvings in stone spells and runes. The roofs of the towers were once shining silver and gold were now green. She stopped in the cool shade to look at some of the runes closer. And she thought about how high these towers once were and how close the water was now. She wondered whether these towers ever rang battle bells and how water was their only enemy now. She laughed to herself how she see wanted to see the past and how those people would probably want to see the future over a thousand years. It would be nice to trade the knowledge, present for the past. Can you control time travel like in the movies? Ali had no idea where and when history was recorded by main points milestones, inventions, rebellions and revolutions, so the best bet was that it would start at one of those points. Which point in history could repeat itself? She shook herself mentally and pressed onwards. The warm sun and light sea breeze helped to clear her mind.

Passing through another tower, she was stopped by a guard for 'ID please' called the tall guard standing up from a large desk 'Random check are increased because of the crash' the confusion instantly cleared and Ali handed over her papers. He scanned them, 'You may continue,' he waved.

She could feel she was being watched as she passed over the shadow bridge. The dark stone seemed to absorb light, it had watchtowers, though not like others, these were built after the fall of Atlantis, made of the same black rock as the bridge. The High Rock itself looked like a mini-castle with towers of different heights, with fires at their spires that never went out. She knew there were more guards on top of the towers from her own guard duties. *Not a bad job*, she thought, thinking back, no action besides the drills, chatting with friends and making new ones at the job while trying to keep each other awake through the early morning half of the night watch. Now they will have something to watch for.

The investigation was still ongoing, nothing was certain anymore, not even her own future, not her teams, not any future. She let out an exhausted huff, frustrated. This was crazy, can't time run backwards? Though maybe it would be a good thing for the clock to go back. Maybe they could erase what happened, what is going to happen.

She reached the library without any more ID checks but guards had been placed outside the library.

'Sorry miss, but you can't go in. The library is closed,' ordered a young shadow guardian but still a shadow.

'I need to go, it's kind of important, plus I have scroll to deliver,' Ali replied politely, hoping she would not have to into details but checking up on what an oracle tells should be valid.

The library of Atlantis is the closest thing to the fountain of knowledge on earth. Pretending defeat, 'Alright, I guess I could come back later.' She calculated in her mind thinking how much better it would be to collect some books now and read later.

The Shadow's radio crackled. 'Get in here now,' growled a deep voice of someone. Forgetting her, they ran in. No harm in having a look, the library was clearly opened now Ali mused to herself. She pushed through the front door. *Is the history section was up on the 11th floor or 12th floor?* She thought, she asked a Librarian. The quiet and peaceful library she was expecting failed to greet her as she stepped into a library standoff.

A standoff in a library, not that the great front hall was not grand or big enough to accommodate a small battle, Ali couldn't deny the fact. The library, the fountain of books, no longer flowed with books scattered over the floor. Samdar and his grandson Samar stood behind the main desk, with scholars and librarians behind them.

'We will do no such thing,' shouted Samar.

'Where do your orders come from?' asked Samdar.

'High places. Now hand over the books and orbs. It is Atlantis we are trying to protect. We can't keep the information about the city so freely available,' growled the leader of a group of shadow guardians, judging by his robe.

'You see, I am not in the business of keeping information and knowledge from people unlike you lot, so you won't mind if I call the high council on this matter, will you?' Summarised Samdar reaching for the phone on the desk except the leader hurled a little electric ball at the phone, destroying it.

'Rude,' harrumphed Samdar. A little fire started on the desk with a wave of his hand, Samdar put it out. 'Ali dear, how may we help you?'

'The history section and I have a scroll for delivery,' she blurted out, the last part of her sentence trailing as she looked around. Well, at least she didn't say time travel, her mind clocking the response. Still dumbfounded by the scene

'Of course, it's on the 11th floor,' smiled Samdar.

'By order of the shadow, hand over what we ask for Samdar or we will arrest you all,' ordered the shadow leader, signalling for his guards to take their places closer.

'And by the high council of Atlantis, I order you to all leave now or you are banned from the library permanently,' Samdar challenged.

Ali almost smiled at the last threat but Samdar was not backing down. If bans and library fines were all he took to face down Shadows, then fair justice to him. A ban from the Library was a very serious thing. It meant no orbs or scroll since that was most missions. You would be out of a job very fast but she supposed that the shadow did different secret things.

'Is that all you have?' snickered the leader but Ali saw a flicker of shock, so one point to Samdar. Looks like secret things still involve orbs.

'Right, let's do this.' Samdar rolled up his sleeves, 'Ali, will you contain the fight?' The shadows looked as shocked as she felt a fight in the library?

'Who let her in here?' exasperated, the shadow leader, pointing her way.

'Now!' shouted Samdar.

Ali raised a dome that would trap energy and people enclosed the two groups. Who immediately start hurling globules of fire at each other. Ali still remembered the day here, her class got a tour and a group of people joking about fire got a ban for a month. Now here Samdar himself was throwing fire. He looked fearless but also like he was enjoying himself. While Samar and some of the other scholars looked as horrified as Ali felt. Ali entered the dome to put out fires. Neither team was really trying to hurt the other but subdue nor overpower was the goal. They were still all on the same side of Atlantis in the Great Atlantean Library.

'Arrest her!' yelled the Shadow captain.

The two guards who stopped her at the door broke from the group and rushed at her. Ali stepped back out of the dome as the guards crashed into the wall. The shadows began hammering and slashing it with their swords. Inside the dome, a scholar cried out. She had been hit with fire. Two other scholars were dragging her behind the main desk for cover. The shadows stepped closer, seeing the weakness they were going to lose. This has to stop. Someone has been hurt, Ali's mind raced, it has to end but how? The guards still had not made a dent in the dome, which gave Ali an idea.

She just needed all the Shadows to be in one place. 'Move back Samdar!' Ali yelled. She ran around the dome towards the shadow team staying outside the dome. She needed to be closer to have control. The guards followed as they neared their team, Ali began shrinking the dome to trap only the shadows. *Twelve shadows in total, not a bad catch*, thought Ali, happy her plan worked but holding them proved difficult as they began attacking the dome twelve against one, not the odds Ali liked. The dome lit up where it was hit, flashing colours.

'How long can you hold them?' called Samdar.

'Ten minutes maybe,' Ali puffed, changing her stance and getting comfortable as she could with her arm held her in front of her, holding the dome in place. 'Maybe more if I take some oxygen out of the dome they would have less energy to fight then but I will be drained completely.'

Samdar began shouting orders to the scholars. 'I going to get us to the infirmary and inform the council about this,' insisted Samar supporting the injured scribe with her good arm towards the main door.

'Be careful, they might be more out there,' called Samdar.

'Don't worry, the game is up, Papa.'

'Can they hear us?' asked Samdar, frowning at the dome and its residents.

'Not well, it is a bit like being underwater.' Ali inhaled deeply, sweat was beginning to bead on her forehead. She remembered learning to construct domes and bubbles like this in her training, it was an effective method for holding people.

'This is a distraction that I agreed to be a part of because I needed it to, though it worked out better for us now, it gave my people a chance.'

'A chance at what?' Ali asked, confused about how the fight in the library helped in any way. But she dared not take her eyes off the dome.

'This shadow came in the front door and asked for what they wanted information on the city, maps, book, spell and secret orbs. But that is not their style and no doubt shadow came in here to take these things without permission while kept most of us down here.'

'But what is the point of stealing from the library when it is free to everyone.'

'The shadows like to point out that some kinds of information should not be free but open only to officials. Making some of the orbs in here are not for general use and some orbs have not been unlocked like the twin orbs. The Shadows see that it should be them who unlock them and decide if it okay for the information to be shared.'

'Do you know if they got away with any book or orbs today?'

'No doubt but I have made copies, hid orbs and even sent some away, this is not the first time in history that others have tried to control knowledge nor the first time that the shadows have tried to censor or keep information for themselves.'

The doors burst open another shadow captain came striding across the floor towards them. Ali jumped, *this is ridiculous! We are all on the side*, she thought but she was still ready for more action.

'Ah, Captain Artemis.' Samdar welcomed. 'Your cohort here wants to take out some books, permanently!'

'Samdar, I am afraid that Captain Hayden is only doing his job,' said Artemis.

'And I am only doing my job protecting knowledge and everyone's right to it,' countered Samdar.

Artemis sighed, 'I am sorry, Samdar, I am. Ali, release them.'

'No, don't, I have heard nothing from the council. I want assurances.'

'We are a part of the council, we need to tie up security. You know that these are time strange and turning more so.'

'You stand for secrecy. I want Lunglock and you all gone until I have his word on this matter.'

'So be it, release them now!' commended Artemis, turning to leave.

'This won't be last you see of us, old man,' growled Captain Hayden.

'Hayden!' barked Artemis. 'Captain Alexander will see you now.' Hayden stormed after her team, following but before throwing some draggers their way.

'By the gods,' puffed Samdar, returning to his desk, he sat down heavily. 'See what they took,' he said, waving the scribes away from him.

'Now what?' asked Ali, picking up a broken orb from the scorched marked floor and placing it on the table.

'We keep guard until the council answers.'

'Artemis, he is third in command?' Ali wondered.

'Yes, after Marcus and Alexander, though I don't know why he is here. He commands the Veracity in the Pacific Ocean. Marcus and his Erbus are always on the move, Alexander's permanent base is here. All three together now, the top shadows. So many questions, I hope Maizann is alright.' Samdar began to look pale.

Ali guessed Maizann was the scribe who got hurt, they sat in quiet for a while. For people who live in the shadows, Ali was seeing much more of them than she liked right now. A man in flowing green robes, which could only be the wardrobe of a high council Far Messenger, entered.

'Far messenger Ralph. It is good to see you,' called Samdar.

'I wish I could say the same of you, my dear Samdar,' replied the Far messenger. 'The Erebus has returned with a pressing matter on board, your library will have to wait, Ali,' he nodded, noting her presence, though Ali thought this was not a good thing. No, no, she did not want a post from the council sent by this man. It was never good news.

'The Shadows tried to steal books and orbs, Ralph Far. This can't be tolerated. Chaos can't excuse more chaos,' pressed Samdar.

'You must respect these times, scholar, the council is doing its best. Lunglock can't be away from the temple but sends this.' Ralph Far removed a scroll from his satchel, he presented it to Samdar, facing him with his personal seal.

'This is meant to gratify me,' stuttered Samdar. 'I respect these times by not committing crimes against people and library unlike those who are meant to protect us against such things.'

'Would you like to meet Captain Alexander? I am sure he would have a minute to spare from the temple,' offered Ralph Far.

'No,' bit back Samdar. 'That is not necessary, thank you.'

'In that case, I will be on my way far to go now,' said the Ralph Far, bowing.

'Not far bound but by words,' replied Samdar, returning the bow.

'This is terrible,' muttered Samdar, breaking the seal, which was an ornate key in gold wax.

'The letter can't be that bad, can't it?' insisted Ali.

'Well, that has to be seen but Ralph Far. He is not just a messenger, he gives the council word.'

'A meeting is in the temple in two days, that is all.' Samdar dropped the letter on the table. 'While the Shadows lay siege outside, we must play our part.' Samdar rubbed his face, tiredness showing now.

'That part being?' Ali questioned, not sure fighting back was an option, thinking on the numbers they have.

'Cressida,' Samdar called, 'she is my right hand around here.' A moment later, a woman with long black hair and red eyes that could only be a fae appeared. 'Cressida. It's time to close the doors.'

'But Samdar, the library has not shut its doors in centuries. What of the scrolls and orbs?' shock played across the Fae's face.

'It time to move with the times, as for the orbs and scroll are not safe, Yes, I see the irony here in hiding them myself,' Samdar mused.

Cressida hummed in agreement, then let out a number of short, sharp whistles. They heard back different whistles, replies from different levels and directions. Some sort of code because only two appeared on opposite stairs and approached, another three jumped from different levels and floated down the atrium, landing beside Cressida. 'Fairies, they kill me every time.' Standing, he nodded at Cressida.

'Dominic and Linn with me, Drusilla, Cornelia, and Zack go opposite.' They formed a semi-circle around the main door as Samdar took his place at its centre. They all chanted together in a language Ali did not understand but it felt old, maybe it was as old as the library itself. The great wooden doors, 12 feet high, creaked and moaned. The swirling iron hinges that were not seen closing in living memory came to life. The door shut with a dusty bang and the iron serpent that were once hinges twisted across the door interlocking their opposite pairs. The window shutter followed the same pattern, the chanting continues books, scrolls and orb that litter the floor began to float, piling up in front of the door blocking gaps in the windows. Dust filled the air as the lamps flicked to life, glowing brighter.

Chapter 9
History

'Are all the floors clear?' Samdar Asked.

'Yes, I don't think we even had extra intruders,' Cressida reported.

'Then let the respectful siege begin,' Samdar announced.

'What about Samar?' Asked Ali.

'There is a secret back door with a secret lock, he will be fine,' Samdar insured.

'What about people who need the library or guardians dropping off orbs?' Ali asked, still baffled that she was taking part in a siege.

'Unfortunately, people will have to live without it, besides it is not like we can trust anyone anyway right. As for scroll returns, we will dust off the letterbox.' Samdar returned to his facing his team. 'Normal duty will be halted and guard patrol set up. Ali, you are welcome to leave if you wish but the Shadows may keep for your part here.'

Ali nodded. 'Wait, I actually still have a scroll for you.' Ali started tapping her pocket and digging.

'Ah yes, for I ordered this for my own research, thank you,' Samdar's smile faded as he returned to his desk and a world of words.

*

They headed to the living quarters of the library in the back tower facing the sea. Linn gave Ali a tour of the place, which consisted of a kitchen with not much food but enough to last a two-day siege, bedrooms and washrooms.

Ali was given a room of her own which was a real luxury for her. She had made up her mind to stay. She didn't do the shadows any harm actually but they could come for her on the grounds of defying rank. But she did have more freedom here and she could do all the research she wanted.

Ali chose the night shift, as she couldn't sleep. So much had happened and when the night came, she couldn't stop replaying the events. So many thoughts spinning around her brain. She thought she would be the only one up late but it turned out all the scribes were night owls. She found them in reading corners all over the library when she was patrolling. Cressida invited her to play cards at the kitchen table that evening, she was grateful they accepted like a friend plus she still was not feeling sleepy. But when the morning came, Ali could have slept through a hurricane. She even slept through Samar and Maizann trying to break in locks like some forgot the secret knock. She felt bad for afternoon lay-in, but the scribes seem to be treating the siege, like a national holiday, playing games, relaxing and forgetting work other than an odd patrol. Cornelia even baked a cake, claiming it to be a new recipe to celebrate the siege. It was a chocolate cake with species, Cornelia had Ali with the chocolate which was her favourite but the species added a delightful warmth to the cake.

The next day Ali hit the books, trying to take in everything she could about the people's history, even people's history, on the last afternoon before the council meeting. A book called 'Atlantis through Time' focused on ancient history, then skipping over the fall of Atlantis and the drowned king. It focused on the middle and modern history of her people, including the new Atlantis. She dozed off only a fifth of the way through 'Atlantis Under the Waves', which started promising with the fall of the city and the loss of buildings. Unfortunately, the book turned out to be more about the architecture of the new Merfolk city than history. Ali then got side-tracked with an orb that played Merfolk music, which she found relaxing, so relaxing, in fact, that she fell asleep. Loud humming woke Ali, who jumped in her seat. She stretched groggily and realised she had drooled on the arm she had been sleeping on, *at least it was not was a book*, Ali thought.

'Find what you are looking for?' Samdar asked, climbing the last few steps to the 11th floor.

Ali blinked, closing her book and adding it to the sack on her desk. 'Nope, not really.'

'Can I ask what it is you are looking for?' queried Samdar, picking up the Merfolk orb and putting it to his ear. 'This is a wonderful one,' he smiled.

There was no harm in asking now but not giving everything away, though. She thought that time looping was possible if history worked in a pattern, but for time to really repeat was that something else. 'Is it possible for time to run backwards?'

'Well, am not going to say no but just that we don't know yet. Time is funny to us, it runs forward, linear, but if it's just one great circle, time will in the end repeat. Although maybe time moving back is just an anecdote when we don't learn from the past and our mistakes, then they are back.'

'I was doing some of my own research into orbs, I think it is good not to take things literally and keep to the facts,' Samdar mused.

Ali nodded, thinking maybe he was right, maybe what the oracle said was not to be taken literally.

'How is your team doing?' Samdar asked.

That query brought Ali back to the present. 'They are all good and well except for the captain, everyone headed home for the days.'

'My thoughts are with Captain Philip and all the families.'

*

The following morning, a loud knocking echoed through the library.

'It is time,' Samdar solemnly spoke like a true outlaw handing himself to face court. He moved from the table they had set up in the middle of the floor to answer the door.

'I really don't have time for this kind of thing Samdar, riots have increased in the hidden cities,' rumbled Lunglock, stepping through the gap in the book wall. 'We all need to work together, we can't be fighting here amongst ourselves, Arcwqil Dareghn will act as a mediator for us today.' Ali had only seen Lunglock once from a considerable distance, the man was head of the high council making him a most powerful man in Atlantis. It was so strange to see him in real life. She had grown up seeing him in the front newspapers, hearing on the radio and TV. Right now, she was sitting at the same table as him because of siege, life has some strange surprises, Ali mused to herself.

Arcwqil Dareghn was the leader of the Line, the ancient head of the Atlantis House, which sat above the Council and the Shadows. They looked after the rights of people at the temple and in the old days were said to have the gods at their ears. The house was generally silent as the council could keep themselves in check but the temple was a place of tradition. Arcwqil was the shared leader of the line as they saw themselves equally as is their founding belief, all equal.

Everyone took a seat, Lunglock looked around the table. 'Does the whole library have to be here?' He questioned Samdar.

'They are witnesses,' Samdar replied.

'Hardly partial.' Lunglock summarised.

'When will we start?' Samdar asked, clearly eager to get the gathering over with.

'When Captain Alexander decided it was time to show up for the meeting,' Lunglock mused, displeased at those words, Captain Alexander bust through the door.

'We have serious security issues to deal with,' Alexander barked, crossing the hall and taking the seat nearest Lunglock. 'If I had my way, the whole library would be shut down.'

'Then you will blind people even more, leading to confusion and ignorance of everyone,' pleaded Samdar.

'Ignorance of the enemy is a good thing, especially considering we don't even know who they are either,' countered Alexander.

'I think is safe to assume that our enemy has advanced knowledge and technology already,' said Samar.

'And we should not have a free service open to them for them to fill in any gaps they might have,' growled Alexander.

'Books of that kind do not leave the library.'

'Do you know who read them right here at the heart of our world, then?'

'Knowledge without persecution.' Samdar fought.

'We are being persecuted you fool!' Alexander shouted, slamming the table

'Enough, I will grant Alexander wish all warfare books will be removed from the shelf today and handed into his care, that is final!' Lunglock demanded.

'No!' Stood Samdar.

'You dare question the order from the high council?' said Alexander, now standing too.

'Sit down, both of you!' Lunglock exacerbated. 'This is the final conclusion. We must ready ourselves for the uncertainty ahead.'

'By blinding ourselves, my family has stood by true, recording history from the beginning for all and I will not stop sharing it,' spat Samdar.

'Knowledge can be used for good or evil in the right hands, up until now, sharing all knowledge was trusting, but now we cannot trust anyone,' Arcwqil spoke gravely.

'I will leave when people can be trusted again,' said Samdar. There was a collective gasp from the scribes at those words.

Arcwqil nodded, rising from the table slowly and left, likely returning to the gods of the temple. Lunglock and Alexander moved to follow.

'Alexander, I will give you the books but no Shadow will move through this library, including you, until they are returned,' called Samdar.

Alexander spun around but Lunglock placed a hand on his shoulder. 'You got what you came for,' said Lunglock. Alexander turned and stormed from the library.

Ali helped them move the furniture back. 'I have to head back to the dorm start packing before cause Yuki will be back later today.'

Samdar only nodded as he packed the marked books into boxes. 'Good luck tomorrow,' said Samdar, shaking her hand.

'We will be watching for you,' grinned Samar.

'All the best,' Cressida smiled.

Ali stepped out into the sunlight, though it held little warmth in the early hour. Alexander, Lunglock and Arcwqil Dareghn all spoke at the bottom of the steps. 'Should have used the back door,' muttered Ali and moved down the step as far away from them as she could, heading towards the docks. She could hopefully merge with that crowd of students coming from the temple, likely from their prayer for tomorrow.

'Redfish,' Arcwqil called.

Alexander and even Lunglock left, leaving her and Arcwqil in the middle of the square. 'So what is your plan after tomorrow?'

'I don't really have any ideas at the moment, my team is hoping to stick together, we will have to go to the Volt the day after and see if they have any plans for us.'

He nodded and they walk for a little until they reached the temple steps 'Did the oracles not tell you anything, a clue to a future life?' asked Arcwqil.

Ali laughed, surprised but then again, it was likely the council was looking very closely at all of them now. 'Only a future that is the past.'

'That is still a future, is it not?'

'How can a past be a future, time cannot turn back.'

'Maybe it's not about time but an event that happened before can happen again in another time.'

'Everything changes,' Ali said, sticking to the fact.

'Yes, everything changes but some things can be paused in time.'

'Do you think there will be fighting?' Ali asked.

'I think there will always be fighting like the riots and unease now, but as long as we have good people like you and your team, we have a chance to win, no matter what,' Arcwqil assured.

Chapter 10
The Marked

'Just be yourself,' Ali muttered, trying to calm herself, 'just be yourself' she could not believe it was graduation day. It was a shame her mother and the rest of them could not be here to see it but the airship to Atlantis was expensive and she would return after today for a short holiday. She knew much of her time would be taken up by job hunting, she and her family could not afford to stay out of work long, even if that meant leaving her team and going her own way last option she hoped though.

Her mind called upon more recent memories of Mia wanting to leave for the other world. How would she cope? Would she be safe? On the other side, there would be no one to trust but she was nearly an adult and had the right on their sides to go down whatever paths they chose. She knew everyone in major cities had a piece of their people so Mia would never truly be far from their world. Peace for now Ali knew that the worries would never fully go away focusing on the here and now she dressed worried about graduation again instead.

'Are you nearly ready?' called Yuki, walking into their dorm room. Like a lot of other graduating guardians, they too had chosen to spend last night in Atlantis. Everyone was wearing the same light grey robe and looked nervously at Yuki's boarding call.

Ali finished tying her boots jumping off the bed. Some people around her were still in their beds with Babylon lanterns still burning. *The dawn ceremony will be too much for them or too much partying last night*, thought Ali, feeling sorry for them because last night Yuki told her that the people who organise the event had people whose only job was to make sure students were not late. Ali did not envy the rude awaking that awaited them. But surprised they could sleep at all, especially through the excitement humming in the room. Ali yawned, they had a long night, trying to describe the siege and explain everything that had happened after, to Yuki.

'Do you think there will be time to see the team before we start?' Asked Ali.

'Well, I hope so,' said Yuki. 'Reece and Jenks said they would try to get places standing on the library steps to watch the ceremony. If the captain stayed at home with his family that would be very understandable. My Family is on the Volt side so we won't get to them now but they want pictures with us afterwards smiled Yuki.

They jogged outside and over to the library, but there were already masses of people swarming in the great square, slowing their run to a shuffle through the crowd. Fires were everywhere, lighting the pre-dawn darkness. They followed Rex through the throng of people.

'Yuki, Ali!' someone shouted their names. They turn in the direction of the voice to see Jenks waving at them from higher on the steps. There were a lot of people dodging before they got to their team.

'I remember Jenks and myself were the ones who graduated before this, that day I kept thinking that I couldn't wait to join up with a really experienced team. Then we meet Phillip and he had chosen you two but I am so happy that I never joined the team I wanted to at the time,' admitted Reece.

'Me too,' grinned Jenks. 'I think we are some kind of weird family now.'

'Reece, how do you think I felt with two new guardians and then two new under guardians and a whole new team to train up?' he smiled then sighed, 'I know our first few missions and even the last did not go as planned being a young team is hard but the mission was always finished and I am so proud of you all,' Captain Phillip confessed everyone smiled at him, all of a sudden he looked very embarrassed and looked at his watch. 'I think it's nearly time you two better run over to the stage,' he said, regaining his composure.

'We will see you all after,' said Ali, turning to leave but a council member Councillor Worlan blocked their path, he was quite high in the Atlantis order.

'I am here to remind you, this team will be asked to stand before the council after the graduation to discuss the events of the fallen ship,' he said his voice ringing with authority meeting all of their eyes before he came to rest on Phillip's. 'You, Captain, will remain now on Atlantis until the council has decided your faith for breaking commands.'

Phillip nodded, 'I will take that as no escort is needed then?' asked Worlan, raising a questioning eyebrow. Phillip nodded again. Councillor Worlan spun on his heel and left.

Ali watched him as he walked through the crowd, drawing in breath quickly when she saw him stop to talk with Captain Alexander. The councilman pointed their way and Ali turned, she did not want him coming over here now not on the foot of bad news, remembering what was said of him before, frankly, she would be delighted if she never had to speak to the man again. She had the feeling though, that they weren't the only ones watching them.

'We will meet you, after,' said Yuki.

'Of course,' said Reece, 'we will stand as a team.' He looked at Phillip but he was watching the crowd. *He had obviously seen Alexander out there too*, thought Ali. A bell tolled and the crowd's mumbling grew louder.

'We really have got to go,' said Ali to Yuki.

They had to push through the crowd. 'So much for early flights home,' said Yuki.

'You are right,' groaned Ali.

As they made their way to the centre of the square where all the other undergraduates were standing. Ali looked around. There must have been at least two hundred of them in lines on either side of the great stones. The outer crowd at half a thousand strong had rearranged themselves to form an oval standing on the steps of the volt and the library amphitheatre of sorts. No one was standing on the temple steps save the council and the Line who watched over the graduation every year and made speeches.

Huge stones were placed at the centre for this one day every year from the great stones ruins of the Atlantis that lay under the water. Still wet, the stone acted as a reminder to all who look upon it and thought of the past and what can arise from ruins. A hush rushed through the crowd as Baron Lunglock walked out of the temple to join the rest of the council on the steps. Ali never could keep up with the Atlantis politics but was a close call for his rise to power, another called Julius Shadow, was his rival. Julius Shadow was Captain Marcus' older brother and engaged to Wilvanra Fay. She was a Shadow and the High Guard with light magic. Wilvanra was not there for Lunglock taking steps to the high seat nor could Ali remember much about Wilvanra other than her being the left hand of the council, in other words, if you did something Atlantis did not like, this woman would hunt you down and drag you before the order. She was also close friends with Thea Cross, the leader Lunglock replaced, which may have put Julius at a disadvantage. People tended to like new blood in the high seat but Julius lost and happily retired with Wilvanra not long ago for wedding bliss. That was the last gossip from the mill Ali heard.

The graduation of guardians tended to be a smaller affair with family, teachers and some lower members of the council, with temple priests and priestesses leading the ceremony. Ali could not believe that the whole council was going to be there but it was most likely for a show of force and unity in these uncertain times. Lunglock dressed in flowing robes of blue-grey, purple and gold, he looked around him as if taking in the view, then nodded to one of the council members.

A member in far plainer brown robes handed him a small cup. Lunglock drained the cup before handing it back, *it was most likely to be echoer's potion*, thought Ali. Which could carry one's voice very far. The whole council moved to lower steps to give Lunglock room for his speech and not be so close to the potion's effects.

'Welcome all! And mostly to our new Guardians to be,' Lunglock boomed, his voice ring through the dawning square. 'I know it is a day to be glad but I would like everyone to spare a thought to our fallen brothers and sisters who passed when their ship the Two Tails went down. Answers will be found but I fear more questions will be asked. But we will thrive, we will stand on. The Gods may have cast us aside in jealousy and blinded the peoples of this earth from each other but we have stood strong and will continue to do so. I would like also to call for peace from the anti-human rioters we must not fight among ourselves. We have so much more to gain by standing together than apart.'

Ali could hear prays being muttered for the Two Tails, sadness and anxiety palatable in the air.

'More than ever do we need our Guardians now, so as in past days, let them walk through the ruins and rise as Guardians of Atlantis!'

The crowd clapped and cheered as he descend the steps. The rest of the council took up positions on either side of him. Arcwqil Dareghn and the rest of the Line followed the last, walking down to the ruin stones. They spread out, forming a circle around the stones, keeping an equal distance from each other. Lunglock raised his staff and began to chant. After a moment, the others in the circle joined him. Ancient magic filled the air, Ali could feel it on her skin like another presence. It made her feel lighter like she could breathe full and deep for the first time. Soon the stones began be vibrate and hum like they were singing out then they started to float, hanging just above the ground before they slowly climbed high into the air, twisting and turning as they assemble themselves to form a great arch.

The opening of the archway faced the temple and the sea, the meaning was that as you walked from the temple out into the world, you would have Atlantis at your back and you would stand for Atlantis. The council members moved to stand with Lunglock at the water's edge of the square. Arcwqil Dareghn removed a cup for his robes and filled it with seawater he return to the arch and poured the water over the stones. 'We will stand for what is lost but not forgotten.' Blessing the stone, he and the Line walked through them and back to the temple, climbing to the top. This was the sign that they were a true link to the past, the only ones who walk backwards through the arch, the crowd parted for them. The guardians were a future and they must walk forward, this was also the sign Lunglock needed. It was time Ali blew out a shaky breath as Guardians nearest the temple began to form a line in front of the arch.

'You may all pass through the Arch of Ruins,' boomed Lunglock.

One by one, people walked through the arch, marking them as new Guardians. Nearly half an hour and someone hundred students later, Yuki was next to walk through.

'Good luck,' Ali whispered.

'See you on the other side,' Yuki said, smiling, looking back at her as she walked away.

Yuki turned, a guardian in the blink of an eye, now standing on the other side. It was Ali's turn, so many years of hard work had led to this point in time but as she stepped towards the arch, Ali wasn't so sure anymore, was she really going to bind herself as a guardian to Atlantis forever? *Funny how things never bother until you have to do them,* she thought. Just do it, she willed and forced herself to keep a steady pace. The arch was right in front of her one more step and she would be marked. *This is it*, she thought, now right under the arch and that's when she heard a loud crack. She looked up and wished she didn't. The roof of the arch was splitting, she made it to run but she couldn't move her legs, then the walls of the arch began to tear and crumble.

She fell to her knees, something had hit her in the back of the head. She reached back to feel her head wet, she looked down at her hand to see blood but she didn't feel the pain, she felt tired or indifferent to it, maybe. What was happening? She vaguely wondered. Looking out to the crowd, she saw a different crowd in strange clothes, a different Atlantis. She took in a sharp breath, there were humans on Atlantis, how is that possible? Atlantis looked more different, it looked whole, untouched by the gods, sea and time. The Ancient Atlantis.

Slowly taking in the scene and the people, Ali realised she was at the centre of this crowd with another, a woman her age, if maybe older. The crowd drew closer, wary Ali looked at them again, realising most had drawn power and some carried weapons. The women drew power too and the crowd from all sides rushed at her. Ali screamed to warn her but she raised her hands above her head and a light shot from her hands into the sky. The crowd was nearly upon them and Ali screamed again, drawing power to protect them. The women looked over at her, seeing her for the first time, then the women became consumed by the light and everything went white.

A different crowd, a different Atlantis, how was this crowd different? Ali was puzzled. They were still running where she was, her hands hurt and were covered in blood. Looking back up she saw the difference suddenly, the crowd they are running away! They are screaming and running away! The ground was shaking. Slowly, thoughts so slow, *was this an earthquake?* That could explain it but Atlantis hadn't shaken since the city was drowned all those long centuries ago.

'Ali!' someone screamed she looked around to see Yuki running and stumbling towards her, she looked petrified. Why is Yuki so scared?

Other people were running to her, council members mostly even Lunglock was on his way over, things must be bad if Baron Lunglock was running. The earthquake that's it, the ground was still shaking. 'Ali!' shouted Yuki again. She was nearly here. Yuki knows what was happening, Ali smiled up at her. Then one of the council members grabbed Yuki, holding her back 'No stop, by the drowning king stop, we are trying to stop her.'

'No!' Yuki screamed and tried to fight the councillor.

Who are they trying to stop? Thought Ali, her thinking was still pretty slow, gloopy like syrup and blurred. With the arch broken on the ground all around, she had a perfect view to see a circle of people forming around her, high members of the council, Alexander, Marcus, Artemis, their teams and other shadow teams. She could feel them all drawing power. Ali could feel more power joining them as The Line ran down the temple steps six, men and women she has never seen them leave the temple at speed, something must be very wrong.

'Cut her off from the air!' shouted Lunglock.

Suddenly, Ali was enclosed in a force field. She could feel that the dome was airtight and that oxygen was being pulled out. Ali thought that if she just stayed calm and called for help but parts of her mind no longer worked and all she knew right now was that some of the most powerful people in the world were trying to suffocate her. She pulled on power, using it to push the force field away from her until the dorm grew and she could feel the people on the other side of it still pouring power into it. The air was getting thinner and thinner and the make matters worse, someone had lit a fire in there with her meaningless oxygen to go around. Now was a good time to panic, *By the Underworld, yes!* She thought. Pulling on more power, the dome grew again, nearly meeting its makers before it shattered, sending shock waves out.

Ali was hit again, this time she knew what it was, the delayed pain was making itself feel. Suddenly, she knew she was never going to feel pain again, this was her last breath. She looked up to see the sky and let out her last breath as a scream. Releasing power, she didn't know she was holding on to.

Part Two
Atlantis Rise

Chapter 11
Fool's Gold

Well, at least I died under the open sky. It was the Sylph's way to die, Ali accepted. Sylph souls would be free to fly on the earth's winds forever. I am awake but is death is another kind of awake right? Who was she, exactly? Ali wondered. I am thinking, do souls think? What about my other senses? Do I still have those? And memory…By the gods, what did I do?

All at once, her senses came flooding back. She could hear, see, feel, and smell. By the drowned king, did her throat hurt! She tried to speak, but only managed a painful choke. She could feel by the air that the room was deep in the earth and the thought of being unground made Ali feel sick. Sitting proved the room to be more of a dark stone cell ringed with Babylon Lanterns. Thankfully, she was dressed wearing some kind of itching hospital gown. The room did not provide any other clothes or clues as to where she was. Ali listed the two possibilities in her mind: she could be under Atlantis in the cells under the temple or taken to a secret base which could be anywhere.

Then, of course, her mind jumped to the why she was here, the earthquake that was me, the explosion that was all me? Ali's breathing became shallow and fast, her chest heaving. Did I hurt people? What did I do? Ali pushed the sheets back to make a break for the only door but one leg caught in the sheet and the other refusing to support her crumpled and she fell. The movement opened up cuts on her hands, arms and legs which bleed through bandages and fresh blood leaked from a gash on her forehead.

That's blood, that a lot of blood that's mine, I am bleeding! Ali's mind registered in mild panic. She gulped in the air and tried to draw power to steady herself but as she did the Babylon Candles burst into flame, taking the power from Ali, the power grab stole Ali's breathe, she pulled more power to keep breathing.

The door. She needed to get out. She limped over, half covered in blood and half tied up in a sheet. She turned the handle but was locked, Ali pounded on the wood. 'Help, someone,' her voice cracked and broken.

'Help me, please, I am awake! The candles, they won't go out!' she screamed. She banged on the door again, with no energy or breath to scream this time. They were going to kill her.

Babylon Candles are not meant to do that they only take the power flairs of a sleeping person, the excess energy that the unconscious throws out to keep them and others safe by burning it off, only children, troubled sleepers and the powerful use them. They were suffocating her. She needed to put them out, pulling power to set them off but she couldn't stop now or she would be snuffed out. Destroying them was not an option. Babylon lanterns had to be opened and drained very carefully.

Energy feeds off energy. *If I could link the candles together, they would burn each other out instead of drawing from me*, she thought. She felt dizzy and her throat began to hurt more, *she must hurry*, she thought crouching down that the closest lantern. She opened the little metal and glass door, letting the energy flow into the room which cause the other lanterns to brighten, Ali felt a strong tug more power being taken from her. She slowly reached in and removed the candle, it was red. Ali had never seen a red candle before they can come in blue, green and cream but never red. Now link them, it was a simple spell to light a candle with another. This candle felt strange in her hand, unlike any other she brought to the centre of the room, kneeling. Ali saw the blood not running the way gravity intended but upward, towards the upheld candle. The blood climbed the candle to the flame, turning it red.

Ali screamed, dropping the candle and started to shake, stepping away from it. This red candle was made with her blood. She turned slowly, all the candles in the room were red.

She ran for the door again, pounding but the candles grew brighter. She threw energy into the door but it only bounded back into the room knocking over a lantern, it cracked and leaked its own energy, surrounding candles greedy flared. Blood magic, the words crept into her mind, an evil myth that was taking on a lethal reality.

Any power she drew for breaking out would be taken from her by the candles. Ali paused, what if she could get them to burn out before they killed her? Breaking all the lanterns at the same time would likely cause an explosion, plus the fact they were hard to break, too. She couldn't just throw energy around the room. Babylon Lanterns are made from metal and glass infused with energy to store energy. Linking was now also out of the question since they were all linked to her. The lanterns store energy, slowly feeding the candle. If she opened them all, it would only accelerate her death. Maybe an explosion was a good idea, the chain reaction meant more energy, not just hers if the candle burned the rebounded energy maybe they would take all the lanterns energy. She picked up the closest lantern and threw as hard as she could against the wall, the candle brighten meaning it took physical energy now too, not just magic. Picking it up from the floor, she examined it, not even dented.

Ali started to cry, kneeling she grabbed another lantern placed on the floor in front of her and raised the other above her. She brought it down, feeling magic pulse when they hit each other but no break. Crying as hard with little breath, she needed to stop, Ali hit the lantern off each again. Only the candles pulsed this time.

Ali stood and hurled the lantern at the door, adding power to her throw. To her surprise, it exploded and sharp pieces flew across the room. Ali dropped to the floor but still felt the shrapnel embedding into her skin. There must be a protective spell over the doorway. But was one less candle but Ali was still running out of time there was at else 20 lanterns left and breaking one took a lot, she didn't have time to break them all. She needed one big explosion, which had to be better than dying a slow death.

Ali sat on the edge of the bed, trying to control her choked breathing, running through the possibilities in her head. Do I pile them in front of the door? It might break it down or if the explosion is larger, then it could trap me, Ali debated. Ali decided lanterns together in a corner near the door. It felt strange tossing them, they were valuable things and to be treated with respect. But they were killing her. In the opposite corner, Ali took her place with one lantern. She drew power and as much breath as she could, the candles of her blood flaring.

Bang! Ali's own power came flooding back to her just in time as things started to fly and a fireball bloomed. Ali instinctively drew a shield but was still forced back against the wall. The room was black and the bed was on fire but the door was open. Well, on closer inspection, it was gone but Ali couldn't leave the room without looking for the candles. The Babylon Lanterns were a melted ruin, too hot to touch, some of the metal still liquid she felt no drain, so hoped there were no candles left, all burned to oblivion.

Ali stepped out from the small cell into a vast circular chamber cast in a deep blue light. Ali had the strangest feeling like she was at the bottom of a well. Looking up to the blue ceiling, she realised it was glass and she was now underwater, of course, she was underground in Atlantis really meant underwater. At least she now knew where she was, simple navigation here. She finally managed to untangle herself from the sheet, dropping it in the cell doorway. The chamber was ringed with doors similar to her cells and large doors on the opposite of the room. At the centre of the room, stood winding stairs way rising through the glass ceiling. 'Two ways out,' she clocked, stepping towards the stairs one of them must be connected to the pool in the temple the entrance for the Merfolk.

"Click." Ali looked down and saw she was standing on a golden band on the floor that ran the whole circumference of the room, some kind of seal, she guessed. Then Ali had a sinking feeling that she had just broken it. Another *"click"* as Ali stepped off the band, suddenly, water began to pour down the walls of the chamber. The water slowly crept down the walls, touched the dropped sheet, which was beginning to burn and dissolve. Ali screamed and ran toward the stairs but not before the smell of burning fabric and blood reached her. That was not water and nor was she going to stick around for a pH test.

Another golden band on the floor halfway to the stairs, Ali jumped as far over as she could, hoping to delay breaking the seal once she touched down on the other side. It would likely trip something Ali did not want to know. *"Click."*

The stairs broke away from the floor and began to swirl upwards without her. 'Aaah!' Ali screamed, throwing herself at the last step. Now dangling, Ali pulled herself up as the water began pooling below. Ali ran up the moving stairs, the water was halfway up the wall, she hoped her opened cell might buy her some time but likely the traps were designed for escapees. Ali, still running for life, did not realise she stepped on a golden step until it was too late. *"Click."*

Ali grabbed the hand railing higher as the golden step and the stairs below her fell into the deathly solution. Once again, Ali dangled from the stairs struggling to pull herself up, she looked down the pool, it was no longer still but seemed to have gained currents and a life of its own as it slopped and swirled, waves build and reached for her legs, not touching yet but spray burned her legs she shouted out in pain. A couple of whirls pool began to form, now did I just see something move down there. Ali pulled herself up and began to climb the stairs, watching out for gold. The stairs wove through the ceiling into a glass tube completely surrounded by water. Now Ali could see the seabed, fish, and coral-covered ruins.

The light became brighter as she climbed and moved upwards but the corroding water was rising to fill the tube below. A metal clacking sound filled the air and to Ali's horror, she saw higher steps at the top were being folded away, leaving her with no place to stand. She hurried on and found a wooden door the stone way flanked by two giant turning spools which the handrail was being spun on to. Here Ali at the top could feel the magnetic pull of the steps be pried apart and slotted into stone shelves. Ali stepped from metal to stone as her step was pulled away. The handle was golden. She wanted to cry, the steps behind her were still disappearing, the water still climbing. What would happen if she touched it? She had come so far to realise that she could never escape. *Cruel of someone to give her hope*, she thought.

There has to be a way through, she looked at the hinges of the door but they were gold too, she could still touch the wood, right? Ali banged on the door. 'Help me, Help!' she screamed. It was worth a try but whoever did this was likely not answer her plea now. Clawing at the door now and crying, Ali stopped and looked at her fingernails and the claw marks on the door. *What about a door within the door?* She thought. *Could she spilt the wood with air?* She didn't know but it had to work.

She drew the shape of a miniature-arched door within the original with air, repeating the shape again and again until under her hand she felt the wood crack. The air on the other side pushed through until she could hear the water sloshing closer. With a good outline made and air going through in places, Ali focused her energy and blasted a small door.

She climbed through into a cramped stone tunnel. The rock itself gave off a slight glow, enough light to see the tunnel leading away from the tube. Ali kept her head low and ran, this tunnel must lead under one of the main buildings. A moment later, Ali felt the air shift. The acid was in the tunnel now. One turn later, the tunnel abruptly ended. Stone stairs with up the only option she climbed on. She felt the water enter soon after her, the stone domed above her with gaps letting light pour in, real pure air, she was at the surface could feel in the air. Ali pushed at the stone but it remained solid. There must be a trick to the stones like opening a secret grotto in a novel. But Ali didn't have time for puzzles, her brain was scrambled. Ali pulled power, she had lifted a lot heavier things before like the airship last week. She encouraged herself and blasted a hole through the stones. Clambering through a hole but there was no solid ground on the other side and she fell into the water. Water that did not burn but soothed her legs, Ali came to the surface, realising she was also very thirsty but also in a fountain in the middle of the Atlantis high court right under the high table. Of course, they were in session and everyone had something to say about this. Voices from every direction shouted but Ali only recognised one.

Chapter 12
Before All

'Ali!' Yuki screamed, running towards her, much to some guards' disapproval, they followed. Ali looked at the hollow fountain and saw new water pouring from the gaps. She pushed her body once more and wading to the side. She threw a burned leg over the side but too weak fell back in. Yuki was at her side, now reaching for her.

'No, Yuki, get away from the water, it's bad it will burn you.' But she began climbing in any way before a guard snatched Yuki from the side.

Two more guards grabbed Ali, hauling her out and dropped her at the edge. She led back against the edge, which the fountain flowed generously now. Finally, she caught her breath and closed her eyes, she didn't care about the voices. She was alive even if it was just for a trial, still, she was not sure not about what happened at the ruins, a trial was better than a cell.

'By the drown city, Silence!' boomed Lord Lunglock, 'Captain Alexander, you assured us she was secured. Why was she not in a cell and why was she swimming in Poseidon's scared fountain? which is now damaged.' he turned his hard look in turn on her. Ali looked back at the fountain. It was still half there, though Poseidon was now missing some stone sea horses, turtles, and mermaids.

'An impossibility seems to have occurred and I request that the council let my team take her off Atlantis, for everyone's safety.' Captain Alexander demanded and managed not to answer a single question, Lunglock returned the favour by ignoring the request.

'Ali of the Redfish, what is the meaning of this?' He asked sweeping his gaze back to her.

Ali struggled to stand, she may not look her best but she would try to stand strong. 'Well, I was in a cell below but there were these red Babylon candles suffocating me. I had to put them out then my cell door exploded with the

Babylon lanterns,' Ali blurted out in a rush so much for strong a real solid answer Ali berated herself internally, at least she kept the blood magic, she dare not say it, best to stick with facts avoiding speculation.

'There no such thing as red Babylon's, my council,' interrupted Captain Alexander.

'There are, they were made from my blood! They're down there in the cell.' gasps erupted from the crowd. She must have sounded mad and she realised there were no candles left down there, the lanterns, what could the corroding water do to them?

'Silence, No more interruptions from anyone,' called Lunglock staring at Captain Alexander. 'Continue,' he prompted, turning back to her.

The water, they would believe that it was sitting in the fountain right beside her, the burns on her legs proof too, Ali thought, gathering evidence in her mind. 'On leaving my cell, I set off the alarm and the whole cell chamber became to fill with this corrosive water, I had to run for my life and the stairs lead up under the fountain here.'

'So we have seen,' muttered Counsellor Samgy.

'Captain, what is this water she speaks of?' asked Counsellor Onlex.

Captain Alexander sauntered over to the fountain, reaching a cupped handed in and drank the water. Ali stepped away from him in shock, the water had burned her. Right?

'I am afraid this is a complete fabrication. Perhaps an overactive imagination developed by one alone in a cell. The wounds are self-inflicted yesterday's injuries exacerbated in an escape attempt.' Alexander shook his hand dry, waved it in Ali's direction, indicating her bloody bandages. 'As for the latest burns, they are clearly the work of Babylon fire,' the captain spoke with pity and returned his spot before the high table.

'I would hardly call it an attempt since she succeeded Captain,' snapped Lunglock, Alexander cringed but stood his ground.

'I can't remember the last time that fountain flowed,' said a fantasised Counsellor Salnari. Half there but still beautiful, the fountain was made from white marble turning green with time.

'Redfish, any final words?' Lunglock preened. He drank the water. How is that possible? Did I imagine it all? I am in the wrong? Ali was still in shock be she needed to keep to the truth.

'I do not deny leaving a locked cell but I was suffering. If water was not intended for burning, then it was for drowning.' Her honesty won her some favour among the councils or was that pity? Nor was all convinced Lunglock was unreadable. The flowing fountain clearly spoke volumes, water levels capable of drowning clear. Ali couldn't help it and she bit back a laugh, this was crazy.

'Ali of the Redfish since you are capable of standing, you will stand trial for yesterday's earthquake and the use of uncontrolled power,' declared Lunglock. 'But first, the court will break, guards take Ali to the infirmary and someone clean up this mess.' They did not use her real name, just the working title of Atlantis, a good sign? Ali did not know as she was led away.

No such thing as mind readers but it would be handling now they could see everything that happened from her view. Ali struck herself with an uncontrolled power that was partly true but the earthquake, surely they were not going to pin that on her, were they? Well, she did not kill anyone by the sound of things, which was the best bit about her charge.

Ali relived as they entered the infirmary. Where she was greeted by a doctor and nurse, burns treated plus fresh bandages and clothes, once she was given a general health check, the doctor nodded to ever-present guards. At least they let her dress behind a screen. Ali was beginning to think more clearly, maybe it was being clean and someone qualified to say you're alright was definitely assuring and life-affirming in this kind of situation. Not that Ali had any kind of previous experience, she doubted anyone had. The doctor and nurse left, she thanked them but didn't get their names.

'Councillor Kqean will act as a judge on this matter, as voted by the high council,' announced Lunglock. The now Judge Councillor Kqean sat at the far end of the high table, closest to the east, closest to the light. Ali noted, remembering some Atlantean law.

'We will commence,' ordered the new judge. 'Reading of yesterday's events and confirmations by the witnesses gathered here today. We will bring the truth to the light. All corrections and differences on the event will be recorded equally,' spoke sombrely Judge Kqean.

Ali looked around the hall there must be over a hundred people here, a couple of people from her year, Captain Alexander and his team, a full high table of eight councillors, the empty High Guard chair and Captain Marcus and the table beside them. The lower half table was full of temple scribes, at least thirty guards, not including the temple guards, which flanked the three exits in the south, east, and west of the building. Finally, in front of the table on the left-hand side of the temple, there was the Merfolk pool directly opposite the fountain. Then the hall was clear for the public or those called to court like today. While her fate lay in the hands of those who sat behind tables on high in the north wing. Finally, sitting above them was the Atlantis House, all seven thrones representing their lines of power. The seventh site always remained empty, as it was the seat of humans. These six people sat in silence over all council matters, making sure all peoples were represented equally. She vaguely remembered them running down the temple steps. They must hate her for threatening Atlantis, their heart of the world, the home of all.

Ali really knew no one but Yuki and a few classmates, she wondered where the rest of the team was, what of her family, her mother and brother and sister, what going to happen? Ali flushed with worry and something that felt like fear.

'At dawn, yesterday seasoned students came to graduate under the ruins of Atlanteans passed. The ceremony started as tradition had seen, Yuki of the Redfish was the last guardian to pass through the ruins. She will speak now,' said Judge Kqean.

'Yuki of the Redfish, I call upon you to stand before this council and speak the only truth.'

Yuki stepped for the high table. 'I will only speak true for the honour of Atlantis,' Yuki promised and bowed for the tables.

The judge nodded and waved the clear glass Atlantis septor of truth in front of him, a sign that he recognised her word, sealing the oath, binding her to it and protecting himself from lies, should the oath not be spoken true. It was said that the glass would crack if lies were spoken, Ali was remembering more myth than the law now but the glass was symbolic of transparency and purity.

'Tell this court what you saw that dawn,' instructed the Judge laying the septor back on its golden velvet cushion. Ali cringed, not sure about that colour anymore. The effect of the adrenaline was beginning to wear off and Ali was not feeling quite so lucky anymore. She was on trial in Atlantis, the centre of their world, surrounded by the highest and most powerful. Her best friend was about to give a statement and she broke their fountain plus some other laws apparently, but that was still vague to her.

Yuki glanced her way before speaking, 'Ali would never hurt anyone she a good person and a great guardian.'

'We are here for facts, yesterday facts only, a person's previous acts do not exclude them from acts they commit later,' rebuked the judge. 'Do you understand Yuki? If not, you will forfeit your chance to speak.'

Yuki nodded and continued, 'I saw nothing out-of-order yesterday, high council. I was marked before Ali and saw nothing unusual about the arch when I walked under. I took my place on the other side and waited for Ali, as she stepped under I heard this low rumbling sound and the arch cracked and began to crumble. I saw Ali get hit by some of the rock and then I ran to help her.'

The judge raised his hand, signing Yuki to stop, 'Can you just confirm that you felt no power surge before the arch broke?'

'Yes, Ali did not pull power, the arch, for whatever reason, broke of its own accord.'

The judge nodded at that response. 'Please continue with the rest of your statement.'

'The ground began to shake and I did not reach Ali as Councillor Rosalind held me back.'

'Councillor Rosalind, can you confirm this?' asked the judge.

'Yes, I can,' said Rosalind, who was seated beside Councillor Esmeralda on the other side of the high table. 'Baron Lunglock wanted us to secure the area.'

'I was pushed out of the secure area and couldn't see much. Then, Ali broke through the circle and I was knocked over by the power surge,' Yuki concluded quickly.

'Thank you, Yuki, you may return to your place,' indicated the judge. Ali wished she had a seat. She was feeling the burns more and yesterday's injuries seemed to come alive with their origin story. Things were still hazy from her side of things, gods she still didn't know if she hurt someone or not but she really hoped not.

Classmates, she knew and didn't who graduated, and didn't come forward giving more or less the same story as Yuki. They all saw the arch fall but it was not Ali's magic. Most of them could also pinpoint the power surge that came from Ali after the arch broke.

Secret guardians spoke next to Captain Alexander similar story to others but one exception.

'I and my entire team, plus Captains Mortimer and Hayden teams, can confirm that the epicentre of the earthquake was Ali.'

Ali all most fainted at that. She couldn't have been responsible for the earthquake, she did not have that power, only air, now she was feeling short on that.

'Thank you, captain but they will all have to speak for themselves under oath,' said the judge.

Before the judge could call upon any more of Alexander's crew, Lunglock raised his hand. 'This court will take a short break,' he said with a wave of his hand. Ali was surrounded by four guards and taken to an anti-chamber behind the high table.

The guards remained, they didn't seem like the chatty type so Ali asked to see her team. The silence remained, so Ali thought to change tack to more basic requirements then. 'How about food and water? A bathroom break is also needed.'

One of the guards left the room. 'Is that a no?' she called after him. *Well, maybe that's how you get rid of them, some privacy would be nice too, screens don't shield crying*, thought Ali. A moment later, the gone guard returned with more guards. 'This way guardian,' spoke the gone guard and led her out another door into a corridor after a couple of turns. She was shown a bathroom and then lead deeper into the temple. They had called her guardian, did that mean she graduated? She did pass under the arch in a fashion.

Another corridor and a richly decorated room. This one, however, contained half the council, Marcus, Alexander and their Shadow crews. Wonderful. She didn't know that Marcus had a team but then she supposed that even shadows had shadows, they wore robes similar to Alexander's crew but they wore a black eagle clasp, keeping their high collars tight around their necks. They were a show of power, the council were well able to look after themselves but the effect they were going for worked, these shadows did not blend into the walls. Ali was not sure what to do, stood as straight as she could and folded her hands in front of her. Silence and all eyes on her, she did best not to meet any, but the walls were not exactly blank either, nope just a nice tapestry of Shadows surrounding them, Kye gave her the slightest of nods. Should have dropped that ship in the ocean, Ali looked away.

'Any outcome of this trial and your fate is limited. Should it turn in your favour, choices for you are still limited,' spoke Councillor Kqean gravely. Fate sounded like a death sentence and choices sounded like she would not have a choice in the matter.

'We need you to think about what is coming next. Should you be cleared and choose to remain a guardian, you will have to leave Atlantis,' said Marcus. Ali was confused so I am a guardian who can't guard Atlantis and if am not cleared, is that jail time? The judge was right not to have many options here.

'Where will I go?' said Ali trying to remain positive.

'That is for the council to decide but it will likely to a shadow base of Atlantis, of course,' replied Marcus.

'What about my family, can I see them?' Fear crept into Ali's voice.

'Not for the time being. Atlantis is on lockdown,' said Lunglock 'It's time for us to re-join the rest of the council.' He held a door and most fled out before she noticed Councillor Esmeralda.

'Wait! Councillor, Esmeralda, I wanted to thank you for saving me.' Ali rushed.

'Don't thank me yet,' Esmeralda said, gathering her robe and leaving. Did that mean she had a friend on the council or that she was on death row?

'What about my crew, can I see them?' Ali asked Lunglock. He pointed to the door as she entered and in walked her team.

'We can't have you eating alone can we?' mused Lunglock, other council members did not look as pleased but left them to have a few moments together with exception of guards.

'Thank the gods, you're alright, they won't let us see you, even your family has been stopped from coming to Atlantis,' said Yuki, hugging her more hugs from Reece, Jenks and even the captain.

'Yes, they said Atlantis was on lockdown, is everyone alright? What about your family?' Ali reviled to see her team but worried for them too.

'Yes, everyone is fine and all visitors are being held on one of the dorm islands. They are questioning everyone.'

'The place is crawling with Shadows. I didn't even know we had that many.' Reece shivered at the word shadow.

A cook arrived with sandwiches and soup and they ate around a small table together but Ali didn't really taste anything, her senses and mind nearly overloaded. 'Just like old times,' grimaced Jenks.

Could be the last time? Thought Ali.

'What happened, Ali?' asked Phillip.

'I don't know, I just remember waking up in a cell.'

'I didn't know we had underwater cells,' Yuki whispered.

'A shadow secret,' Ali guessed but there were secrets that should be reviled. Ali didn't get time to tell them when a bell tolled and the guards took her away.

The trial continued with councillors coming down from the table to speak under oath all equal in law and glass. Once everyone had spoken, judge Kqean stood up and cast the glass over himself.

'The people of Atlantis have spoken, on hearing every word and seeing all equal the story has been told, your faith sealed by them. Ali, it has been decided that you are guilty of uncontrolled power but you did so under stress, pain and confusion. The earthquake may have started at the point you stood. However, it has been determined you are not the cause as it is not in your powers or anyone's range, nor were any explosive devices found so will be deemed as a natural phenomenon.'

Ali couldn't breathe. Guilty, she had committed an act against Atlantis the minute she stepped forward to guard them.

'It seems your team has been involved or related on some level to all peculiar events lately but you and your team have proven themselves. Your guardian title you will not be taken from you, should you choose to remain a guardian. But you will stand outside Atlantis serving but never to return, should you leave this life, then a cell awaits you. Some time will be served, also know this for the damage to the city, you will never return.'

I am a guardian.

Chapter 13

Tower

Ali didn't remember being taken from the temple. She could only hear the judge's words resounding that she would never see Atlantis again. An exile to serve them or time.

Her new cell was a tower base rock, southeast of the main island run by the temple guards. Ali couldn't tell if she was no longer a shadow level threat or untrustworthy to Alexander. The stone tower had a simple guardroom at the base, open stairs and a single room at the top. Hers, for now, there was the small alcove at the top of the stairs with a desk and pulley system, she guessed for food and letters. She didn't care really, but mercifully the cell had a window, bittersweet it was and east facing. She could see all of Atlantis cruel or kind, she was going to memorise the image. Ali unwounded the bandages around her hands, ancient runes from the shattered rock had imprinted themselves onto her skin. Vague memories of blood surfaced, the doctor just called them imprints. She was truly marked now, *not just by stone by the law too, uncontrolled use of power*, she thought. Who would ever trust her again and couldn't she trust herself anymore.

The guards informed her that she would be here for five days waiting on the council's final decision on where she goes with further punishment of no visitors. Too tired to cry, she fell into a deep sleep, she felt safe for the moment in a tower on the edge of her beloved city almost like someone watched over her.

Before dawn, Ali woke and pushed her cot over to the window so she could sit and watch the sunrise. It was the most beautiful thing she had ever seen or maybe because it was going to be one of the last times. Her whole life she wanted to protect Atlantis, to be a guardian now. She brought harm and would never see her dream come true. The view was different in a new light but Ali studied the living map and recalled fond memories. Meeting the team for the first time in the Volt. Her nights on the dorm islands with friends or in the summer they would swim in the sheltered small cove on the island. Walking all the bridges, coming in and out for missions, this place was her home. Her eyes came to rest on the burial island in the west no bridge connect it to another island or the mainland. There were other memories here: failed tests, arguments, doubts, worries, sadness and now graduation.

She looked down at her hands, the ancient ruins they had passed from the stone to her she was still marked. What of her family and friends? What would they think? Would I never see them again? She cried then for a long time until the warmth of the sun hit and lulled her back to sleep.

Knocking on the door woke her. 'Enjoying the view, I see.' Kye's voice came muffled through the door.

'I thought there was to be no visitors,' Ali yawned, stretching her from her nap. She was half sitting in the crumpled bed, having slept on folded arms in the windowsill.

'I am not here to visit,' quieter and more solemn came his reply.

Ali turned around to see a serious face through the door's small barred window. Just another guard turning back, she could see people bustling about Atlantis was beginning its day without her. 'What is happening out there?'

'The lockdown is still in place and clean-up is over, some people are returning home, but I fear Atlantis will not return to normal as quick. The council is still arguing over where to send you. Even The Line is joining the fae, they want you as a High Guard but the council argues you are not ready, too unstable. They want to have your magic retested.'

People wanted her to stay. Hope flickered in Ali's heart but powerful people in a job she knew little about dampened the feeling. 'I thought you were in line for High Guard, Kye Shadow?'

He regarded her with cool eyes, making her think how the captain came by that piece of information. 'I was but Alexander wanted a trade and then you came along Ali of the Redfish.'

'What did he want to trade for you?'

Kye laughed, 'I don't know.' Ali didn't think it was funny, what do you trade power for? More power, all too likely.

'How is your captain?' Ali queried, trying another tack for information.

'Do you want breakfast or not?' he moved away.

Or no tack, she sighed and straighten. 'Breakfast please,' she called out, hoping he heard.

A few minutes later, a hatch in the wall opened a tray was deposited with water and porridge. The rest of the day consisted of Kye trying to mine her for information on the quake but two could play that game.

Evening came and she knew nothing new about the Shadows and they knew nothing more about the quake, mostly because she didn't know anymore. 'Tell me something am allowed know,' she laughed at the door.

Kye was not looking, he had given up looking like a guard and was sitting against the door. 'A shadow keeps all to the shadows,' he growled back in their mantra. She pulled power just a little out of frustration. She wasn't allowed to use magic anymore but the instinct never dies.

A timely change of guards came. 'Wait! What of my family and team? Please, I need to know,' Ali pleaded, she had asked a hundred times with no answer, but she was not done trying.

'I will find out what I can,' Kye relented.

A power she did not know was there dropped, looks like he never stopped being a guard. 'Thank you.' Ali watched the light disappear from Atlantis, leaving only the watchtowers burning.

Another sunrise just caught in her throat a little, but she refused to cry, couldn't let them see her like this and she doubted the guards carried tissues for prisoners. A loud knocking made her jump, by the gods, did this man not fail yesterday?

'Messages or breakfast?' Kye shouted through the door.

'Messages,' she said without a single thought she hoped he didn't really mean one or the other because she was really hungry, surely not the council's style to starve her though hard choices had been pushed on her by them, surely not, her stomach knotted as she jumped off the bed. Any news from the outside world was welcome, the thoughts and voices, her own connection closer than her looking-glass over the city.

Two little envelopes slid under the door and fluttered in different directions. Ali didn't know which one to go after first. She couldn't help it snatching the closest and leaping on the other. The handwriting on them indicated one was from her mother and one from Yuki.

Ali, my dear,

Yuki has told us what has happened but the council still has a ban on travel into Atlantis. Please write if you can and let us know you are safe. The council has only informed us much the same as Yuki told me, only that you were tried and waiting to be sent to a remote base.

With all my love, Your Mama.

Ali wanted to hug her Mama so much but it cheered her a little to see her handwriting. The next letter was definitely Yuki scrawl.

Ali,

The Redfish crew are all still here and missing you. We don't know what the council is going to do with us and I don't think the council knows either, to be honest. We didn't know which tower you are in, but judging by the shadow fleet moving to the south-east side, we are guessing you are on one of the rocks. Can't say much is happening. Only that we would love to see you and that we should be celebrating our graduation and last mission.

Yuki.

Reece, Jenks and the captain signed the letter too. It was kind of nice to know when she was looking out the window thinking about her friends, family and Atlantis, there were people in the city looking for her.

The food hatch open, yesterday's breakfast was repeated. 'Just in case words are not enough,' said Kye.

'You read them,' Ali blurted out just in the way he said it. Ali knew that others had read them, too.

'Not me in particular but others on the shadows council, they have to monitor these things. You are in jail,' he said like he had to remind her.

Ali decided not to respond to this and took her breakfast and reread her scrutinised letters. What did they think her mother was going to say? But there was something about Yuki's letter. Yuki loved crime, mystery and a little bit of horror, any book or movie that rolled these three into one and Yuki was delighted. 'Can't say much is happening' because there is nothing happening down there or there is and she can't say? Plus, their last mission was nothing to celebrate because they violated direct orders in the end. For the captain, for Phillip's brother Ray. *The fallen ship, it was here on Atlantis.* Ali almost choked on her porridge as she folded the letters, best not to bring any attention to them, not if her thoughts were anything more than daydreams. She needed to see something. Standing, she walked into the room with her porridge, she was still being watched.

'For digestion!' she called out, she heard a chuckled and Kye moved away. Ali scanned Atlantis, the water surrounding the city in specific. There! The Erebus and the Veracity docked to the north behind the temple now but there was no hiding these ships. Their size had one downfall. There was still a mystery of the fallen ship and who was the sixth person.

'Kye, will I be able to see anyone before I leave?' Ali called, putting the tray back into the hatch.

Kye looked up from his little desk in the alcove. 'Did your letters tell you anything?'

'Absolutely nothing, that why I want to see people,' Ali smiled innocently as she could.

The council was in deep session until late last night, maybe something will come off that today. He looked past her out the window.

'What happening out there,' she dropped the smile.

'Everything is classified now,' he said shaking a daydream away.

'How did you become a shadow?' she asked, curiosity struck. It's not like it was a thing people could sign up for. Their education simply stated they were selected by the shadow council members of the council and shadow captains.

'That classified.' He moved back to his work and started to shuffle papers.

'Alright, how does anyone become one?'

He looked up, 'They find you or some are born to the shadows, I am both and either, any more questions on the shadows and I will turn your next letters into a jigsaw.' He returned to his papers. Ali drew air in from the window to hit the desk with a micro blast, papers exploded and rained down all over the room. A couple floated out the open door and drifted down the stairwell.

'Ali!' Kye shouted, snatching the paper from the air.

'What? A jigsaw sounds fun now, not much to do here,' she called back through the flutter of paper.

'Ali!' he growled.

'Oh right, that's one strong draft. I will close my widow in here.' She couldn't quite keep the smile from her face. She dutifully closed the window. Suddenly, Lunglock's voice boomed through the tower.

'Kye, why are there papers all over the stairs?' Ali rushed to the little window and Kye rushed to the stairs.

'Just a minute,' Kye called down. 'Damn! This man is like a mountain goat!' Kye exasperated and rushed around collecting paper.

'I could help if you let me out.'

Kye barked a laugh, 'Never going to happen,' and he slammed the paper down on the desk, turning to collect more.

'You know filing is almost like a jigsaw,' Ali pondered out loud, trying not to laugh, especially since Lunglock was marching up here.

Kye turned to glare, 'Ali, I feel so much as a breeze, a stray air current.' He put more paper down on the desk. 'I will have to report you!' The room was still a mess. It would look bad for both of them, without taking her eyes off him she drew power slowly not to alert Lunglock and gathered the rest of the papers up and placed them on the desk beside him. Wide-eyed at first to see the papers flying, but he nodded once they settle on the desk. He knew it was for both of them.

A moment later, Kye greeted Lunglock. 'I believe these are yours,' said Lunglock handing papers to Kye.

'Yes, yes, they are thank you, the windows—'

Kye began but Lunglock raised an eyebrow stopping him, 'I wish to speak to prisoner alone.'

'I am afraid I can't allow that, Sir. My orders are from Marcus. The prisoner must be guarded at all times.' To stand up to Lunglock was something Ali thought not possible but his order came from Marcus, Lunglock's equal on the shadow council. He waved Kye away and approached the cell.

'Baron Lunglock,' Ali nodded in respect.

'Redfish, I have come the see the new chess piece everyone wants on their side of the board and to inform you of recent events.' Lunglock returned the nod.

Ali guessed she was the new piece.

'As of last night, the Line and the Shadows are thinking of joining together against the council's ruling, they want to keep you here,' Lunglock explained.

Ali needed to sit down, The Line was weighing in on her case. Questions flew from, 'What! Why? Do they even have that power?' They should hate me, right? Ali kept that last question to herself.

'If the shadow council joins them, then yes they do, their voices their vote have not been heard in living memory. I am going to be honest with you, they want power, their power is silence they can only speak on matters of traditional law. They have little control and little power. Wilvanra, the last High Guard, took orders from the council but also a link with the shadow council. Her fiancé, Julius, was a member and captain. Though the High Guard is meant to be free of influences and basis that has never happened, it was the first time in history that a shadow became a High Guard. Now The Line is looking to take your power from the council hypothetically, of course, all high guards are meant to serve Atlantis fair and justly.' His eyes flicked to Kye sitting on the desk.

A power struggle and she was in the centre. Some even wanted her to become High Guard, Ali couldn't comprehend it. She just wanted to be a Nav but she couldn't find her way out of this.

'Why take control? Why now?' Ali asked, confused about the Line weighing in on this matter.

'Because The Line believe you are one of them. You are the key, they argue that your uncontrolled use of power was not your fault and we were harsh to banish you and that your powers should be harnessed and cherished. They believe you will be needed, they believe a war is coming between us and humans. Atlantis shaking was their sign and you are at its centre. They will join with the Shadows if they must and take power from the council. They will keep your banishing sentence and prison sentence on the table to control you.'

'But I thought the High guard was solely controlled by the council following the rule of the first High Guard.'

'The kings were powerful and controlled by none, the high council was born after the Drowned king. They saw the power that can be controlled by one person but that same person should not use be soul control. Yes, the high council created the position but no ruling was shared with the Line so they lost power, they had been the second power to the king. Times are changing, the Line wants the power back.'

'You don't want me to become High Guard? You don't want them to have power?' Ali realised aloud. She wasn't sure if she wanted the job either but maybe it was better than banishment or prison.

'The line has many antihuman views. I fear combining them to the Shadows, there is a chance for war and that choice will be made soon, I must return to the temple.' He turned to leave.

'Wait, what happened to Wilvanra?'

'You know what happened? She retired with Cross, the job is straining.'

'Where is she?'

'I do not know.'

'Do you know what is under Atlantis?' Ali called, thinking about the deep cells.

'What lays in the dark belongs to the Shadows,' Lunglock said walking down the steps.

Chapter 14
Bridges

Sleep was proving to be elusive. Ali had more questions than answers. The ruling triangle of Atlantis was turning on itself and she was at its centre. The Shadows and the Line have ruled in balance, with the council being the most powerful as it was closest to the people. But the balance was changing, the future uncertain. Nothing like this had ever happened before Ali flashed back to a mountain covered in mist, the prophecy of time turning back, it can't be repeating itself. *Maybe the prophecy has not begun yet. Maybe it's for the future*, another unsettling thought, could this present repeat itself? Ali hoped the gods would not be so cruel.

Ali caught a movement outside her cell, she called out, 'Any letters?' hoping for a distraction from her dark spiral.

'Not today,' called Kye dropping himself into the chair.

Ali felt very lonely all of a sudden. This could be a bad sign. If the council won, they would continue with the banishment, she will never see her family again. She never got to send them her postcard.

'Can't do anything about letters but you do have a visitor.'

'Who?' Ali asked suspiciously.

'Arcwqil Dareghn of the Line in an hour or so.' Kye went back to his work as if he didn't just drop a bomb. Arcwqil Line, The Line was coming to see her! He was going to ask about the High Guard, Ali couldn't think of another reason other than her destroying the ancient rune stones or the Poseidon's fountain in the temple. Ali, cringing, couldn't decide which was worst. Ali paced, not that she could pick up much speed in the small cell but it helped, she cleaned herself and the cell and then settled in for some nail-biting. By the time Kye got word from downstairs that Arcwqil was on his way, Ali had most of her nails chewed away.

Kye greeted Arcwqil at the top of the stairs and mumbled something to him.

'Yes, yes, I know your orders,' he signed and handed an envelope, 'new orders Marcus will see you now.' Kye saluted in the old Atlantis style and headed downstairs quickly leaving her alone. Arcwqil stared at her through the door for a moment and headed to the desk as he went through a drawer. 'Here we are,' he smiled holding up some keys. 'I try and see people on an equal ground,' said Arcwqil, filing through the bunch of keys. He hummed when he found the right key and opened the cell door, then returned to the desk, easing himself into a chair. Ali just stared at the open door.

'I am being freed?' she asked, inching closer to the threshold.

'No, I am afraid not, I can't do anything about that for the moment but we can sit out here for a while.' This was very strange, Arcwqil visiting and inviting her to step out of jail, how her life had been turned upside down. Is this a test? She asked if she could not quite bring herself to cross over.

He stood and held out his hand, 'Ali of the Redfish good morning and may I extend the greeting from other members of the Line.'

'Hello.' Ali was very embarrassed now. There was no not leaving the cell because it would be the height of rudeness not to shake this man's hand. She shook the old hand and took her seat opposite him. 'I know Lunglock came to see and what you discussed is between you and him. I will not pry, but we need to broach a subject which no doubt came up.'

'The High Guard.'

'The High Guard indeed,' he repeated, nodding. 'A position of immense power and responsibility. You are the first and last line of defence.'

'Why me? I don't think I am right for the job, I don't want power over people. I don't want war,' Ali rushed with honesty.

'You have proven your power before all Atlantis now, it is not about power over people, it is the power to stand between the people and danger. There are grave dangers on the horizon, Ali.'

'If I say no, what happens?'

'That is your choice but the High Council Atlantis has a way of burying its problems. You can't walk away from this, it is jail or work on a shadow base. But hopefully, with the backing of the Shadow council, we can give you another option of becoming a high guard. The time is now, humans will destroy us unknowingly,' Arcwqil sighed sadly.

The choice is mine but it's not much of a choice, only one gave her the most freedom, her mind flicked to Wilvanra. 'Can I think about it?'

He nodded and looked out the window. 'The council gathering continues,' he nodded, 'the third option should be yours by tonight.'

'Will Marcus come and see me?' She wondered about another leader to argue their side.

'I doubt Marcus will come, he is a very busy man but we can also have no doubt that he doesn't need to be here.' His eyes flicked towards the stairs. 'Things are changing in the outside world, things that are going to affect everyone. I fear the Council has delayed too long to deal with humans.'

'How can we help humans, when magic has no effect in their world?' Ali asked.

'They can still hear some of us, we have not faded completely from them, not yet.' Arcwqil stood starting towards the stairs. 'Good luck, Ali.'

Ali stood too but did not follow, she knew who he was talking about, she wandering around, the view from this window was not much different to her except she could see more of the Erebus and Veracity, was it really humans? Her mind drifted. Sometime later, she heard a different guard's sound on the stairs and she ran back to her cell, ditching her plan to let Kye catch her lounging in his chair. She closed the door as quietly as she could. But the guards were not alone.

'Yuki,' she shouted, and nearly wanted to cry. They held hands through the barred window. 'How you are here?' asked Ali, still in shock about who was on the other side of the door.

'The council relented, they said you were going to be free soon away. They said one visitor figured they didn't want us to outnumber the guards.' Yuki beamed, then look confused. 'Do you know what the council meant? Are they dropping the charge?'

'Not quite, more like the Line is giving me another choice,' Ali filled Yuki in on the rest of the details.

'I think I need to sit down,' she looked like she was clutching the bars more in support than shock. 'The line, Lunglock spoke to you and the shadow council is involved? This is crazy!'

Repeating it did not lessen the severity of the situation but it felt good to talk about it, but Ali now needed to know about the world outside. 'What about the team and Atlantis?'

Yuki smiled, 'Have some good news on that the front charges have been dropped, full lockdown should end tomorrow so people will be able to travel like normal and your family should be here the day after, all going well.'

'Thank you, Yuki,' she smiled through damp eyes.

'My family is still here since most people left, they nearly have a guest island to themselves. We can go and spend time with them and the team will come too,' Yuki already planning ahead.

'Sounds really good,' Ali forced a smile. They tried to talk about good things and good times, but a long silence settled.

'What are you going to do?' said Yuki.

Ali felt a twinge of jealousy. Yuki was free and so many other people walk through that arch on that day. Ali felt guilty then Yuki was her friend, she was still standing by her. 'I don't know, if I leave, I will have to serve some time and never see Atlantis again, but I got the rest of the world and I think that is alright. But I don't know, high guards serve for life as a commitment. I know nothing about it. All high guards die at their post, Wilvanra is the only one known to have walked away and Lunglock couldn't tell me anything about her.'

'Well, let's not jump to conclusions, she retired, remember?'

'She was very young to retire,' Ali argued back.

'Maybe they need to change the job description. You serve some time and retire like everyone else unless you are Samdar or you are on the Line,' Yuki reasoned.

They were interrupted by their debate by Kye. 'Dinner,' he announced, walking up the stairs. He nodded to the guards and they left.

'Mm, have they forgotten me?' Yuki questioned, craning her neck as he disappeared down the stairs.

'No, due to charges being dropped, visitors are allowed to stay longer.' He handed Yuki the tray and moved to unlock the door but Ali opened it just before he turned the key. Ali took the keys from the lock and handed them back to him. He hid his shock well.

'Welcome! Yuki, to my cell,' she laughed, stepping aside. Kye bemused, closed the door but did not lock it and returned to his desk. Yuki put the tray down and they hugged each other, nearly crying with happiness. She had her freedom.

'Ali, were you messing with papers!' Kye shouted.

'No' she shouted, holding in her sob. She winked at Yuki, she had a little look earlier, Yuki held in a laugh as they both sat on the bed.

'Not bad, Ali, your own bathroom and a nice view.'

'Now, I have just to deal with the nosy neighbours,' smiled Ali. Yuki laughed and they shared the sandwiches and one cup between them.

It is easier, too easy to talk without bars between people, Yuki regaled more outside tales. 'Jenks and the captain nearly had to sit on Reece when they charged you, they agreed it was unfair as you were not in your right mind and that you saved the shadows, we think that is definitely working in your favour now.'

They both sat with their backs against the wall and their legs dangling off the bed. 'You tired?' Ali asked.

'Ya really tired,' Yuki yawned. 'Must have been all those stairs.' She giggled.

The door burst open and people dressed in black and faces covered rushed in. 'Get her and leave the others,' someone shouted.

Ali and Yuki screamed, scrambling to stand on the bed, further away from the intruders and attempting kidnappers. Ali threw up a shield but the ground was unstable and Ali knew it was not the bed she was standing on. They had been poisoned. Yuki was freezing the air, dropping the temperature to tilt the playing field in her favour. Those with fire abilities did step back but someone with a double-barrelled sliver gun stepped forward, a shield breaker. These guns were designed in defence against people with air abilities, its blast could travel across whole shields, weakening it and combined with other attacks, it could work. Ali's shield surrounded them completely, to not let the energy hit them from behind. Bang! Green energy jumped from the gun surged around the shield. Ali felt the pulsation through her arms and the pressure increase.

Crash! The window smashed behind them and their bubble hit the wall. 'Brake them up!' shouted the same deep voice. Ali could assume this was their leader. She nodded at Yuki. Ali allowed Yuki to send ice daggers through but they melted before they reached him, a fire wielder! The leader threw fireballs at the shield. Ali could feel the vibration as others joined their leader, ice, fire and other forces pounded the shield Yuki tried to put out the fire before they hit. Bang! Greener energy spread across the shield. She could hear Kye fighting but couldn't see him anymore as the room filled with smoke.

Ali screamed but she could not hold on any longer and dropped the shield. She took hold of energy flying that they returned it with some energy of her own.

This pushed the soldiers back and even some out the door. Ali looked at her hands. What did I just do? But there was no time to question the natural instinct. 'Yuki, let break them up!'

Yuki nodded and sealing the door with ice, Ali pushed the remaining three into the corner to wait for Yuki sealed them in.

'It won't hold them out for long,' shouted Yuki, bright flashes lighted up the blue-grey ice. Only one other way out, they both turned to the window at the same time.

Ali grabbed a piece of broken wood and moved the glass away from the sill. 'We are going to have to jump.' The window was too small for both of them, 'who first?' she asked.

'You! Ali, it is you they are after,' urged Yuki, pushing her closer to the window.

'No, there is ledge out here, we can jump together and I will be able to slow the descent.'

Ali climbed out, cringing as glass dug into her back and arms. It was a long way down and their waves crashing over rock at the bottom, a strong wind buffeting her. She tried to draw power to fly but Ali felt the world spinning and couldn't find her footing on the sleek stone. She screamed as she slipped. She could feel every muscle in her body tearing as she dangled from the window.

'Ali!' Yuki screamed.

Yuki had her by the arms and began to pull her back in. Ali tried not the wriggle too much but she needed a foothold. Gravity and her weight felt greater than the strength in her hands.

Bang! Two things happened at once, the tower exploded and Yuki let go. Ali absorbed power to shield her from flying rock and to remain in the air, looking for Yuki. Some people had landed in the water. She drew more power to fight but the leader stepped to the edge of the tower feet away from where she floated. Half the top of the tower was missing but some of the wall where Yuki was standing was still there. The blast was not to kill them. She needed to find her, she could be in the water. The leader pointed his gun at another, who began to move the rubble. Yuki, she was alive! She threw a shield around her dropping her own shield. Ali felt dizzy, she couldn't work multiple energy outgoings. Ali called the wind and it whipped around the tower faster and faster, enclosing it in a twister to distract them and pull Yuki out.

'Stop!' the leader roared and stepped closer to Yuki. Who was walking slowly before he could point his gun at Yuki. Ali dropped the storm but now she was wanted to drop this man off the tower but fear ripped through her, Would the shield hold? She didn't trust the man. She needed to get Yuki the hell out of there. She strengthen the shield around Yuki and began to slowly raise her from the rubble.

'In your own time then,' the leader called, turned the blast gun on her and fired. It happened so fast Ali was knocked halfway to the main island, she barely had a shield in place and the energy burned her, as she flew through the air, she tried to slow herself but she hit the water hard, skipping three times.

The force pushed the air from her lungs and replaced it with water, Ali didn't know which way was up or down. The only thing rising was panic, the water swirled electric green with fizzy white bubbles.

Hands grabbed Ali's arms, hauling her to the surface. 'Will the bridge be alright?' asked a mermaid.

Ali coughed water nodding, there are others in the water her mind racing, *Yuki! Who were they*? But Ali was still winded from hitting the water, she couldn't voice her thoughts.

The mermaid left her on some rocks, which would allow her to climb up on the stone road bridge that connected the outer islands to the centre. Ali dragged herself over the rocks still coughing, she lay on the road for a minute to calm herself. She could feel her blood pulsing in her brain and her ears rang painfully. Cold crept over her body, Yuki!

'Ali!'

She rolled to the side to see a Kye racing towards her, looks like he had been in the water as well.

From the ruined tower behind him, a dark ship was taking off. They have Yuki, she knew it. The air vibrated and the road she lay on hummed, she turned to see Atlantis guards and council members running down the road. She coughed they were getting away! They had Yuki! She needed to stop them! The dark ship was turning away from Atlantis and began to pick up speed. 'They are getting away, Yuki!' she shouted hoarsely them pointing to the ship. Atlantis airship roared over headed 'No!' she screamed. 'They have Yuki!' But the sound of ships overhead deafened them all. The dark ship had a speed Ali did not think was possible but Atlantis ships still gave chase. They all disappeared over the horizon.

'Ali!' Kye pull her up but she pushed him away, still coughing up water.

'You! You are one of them.'

'No! Please, let me explain,' he looked worried at the small army bearing down on them.

'Yes, you are one?' Ali said, still in disbelieve.

'I didn't know they would come for you so soon.'

'You poisoned the food, they took Yuki! You let this happen!' Ali felt enraged and betrayed.

'They have my family, I didn't poison the food but I am not the only one who they have by the throat.'

'Who are they?' Ali asked, 'and why shouldn't I confess everything I know now?' She looked towards the Atlantis guards bearing down on them, their pounding steps shaking the bridge.

'Because they won't believe you and we can get Yuki back.'

'Why should I trust you?'

'Because I believe we can get them all back.'

'What?' she cried as two guards grabbed her off the ground held up her by the arms.

'Get off!' she tried to shrug off the guards.

'Ali of the Redfish,' barked Lunglock, interrupting her accusation.

'The tower was attacked by unknown forces Sir, they have taken Yuki of the Redfish,' Kye reported.

Ali just stared, dumbfounded at them. He should have the guard hanging off him, not her.

Lunglock turned to a young council member. 'Call everyone. We meet within an hour.' The man turned and ran back to the main island bring, 'and I want Alexander out here,' Lunglock shouted after him. Kqean, I want all injured taken to the infirmary and they are to be guarded twice fold, and finally, the Atlantis will remain on lockdown no one in or out.

'The rest of you with me we must stabilise the tower and see what they left behind.'

'They have Yuki,' Ali coughed.

'We will get her back once we knew what we are dealing with. We will call for you from the infirmary.' He pressed.

Ali was marched back to Atlantis while a small army passed her in the opposite direction.

Chapter 15
Ring Fall

Ali wanted to question others from the tower who were brought in but they gave them her own room and more guards. The doctor, the same man from the temple he must be the council's private physician.

'Just a quick check-up the council wants to see you, soon,' the doctor assured.

Ali nodded. She felt okay but it could still be the adrenaline, better safe than sorry, she sat on the bed.

The doctor asked questions and Ali knew she answered but she didn't really hear them.

'I going to run some tests, but I think you are just in shock. They say you were hit with a shield breaker so it's not surprising.' the doctor said with raised eyebrows and left with her chart in hand. *This can't be happening*, she thought, dazed, Yuki is gone.

The doctor returned. 'I can declare you fit. It was a good sign to start with you walking in here but still, take it easy. Got to give your body a chance to rest and your mind too.' He looked back to the chart. 'As for the poison, you were drugged with a sleeping potion but split between two people, it was not enough to knock someone outright, combined with your heavy magic use you will likely feel lethargic for the rest of the day. But that should wear off by tomorrow with a good night's sleep.'

'Are there any side effects when the potion is in your body?' Ali asked, worried about how it might affect Yuki.

'Not that I know, but everyone's reaction to potions is different, you were still able to use magic, so I would take that as a sign the potion will have or leave no side effects,' the doctor concluded.

'Thank you,' Ali said.

The doctor nodded, 'Right, I will leave you then, everything you need is there, in the closet.' He pointed and turned to open the door. 'Plus, the guards will be on the watch just out here, ready to take you over to the temple.'

This was good for Yuki, a small thing she knew. But Ali had to hold on to the small things right now because so far there had been missiles firing, an earthquake, blow up and shot at. But the small thing about the poison that it had no side effects, was good. She wanted to laugh but she was still too tired. Ali changed into fresh clothes from the closet, her boots had nearly dried out, so that was another small thing. Ali was just about to open the door when a knock came.

She nearly shouted and drew power on the seeing the knocker.

'Please, we need to talk, for Yuki's sake,' Kye whispered urgently.

'You weren't just a shadow, you were their shadow,' she whispered, backing into the room.

'Yes, I know there is no trust here but please let me give my side of the story.'

She nodded, barely controlling her power, her rage.

'They have my family.' Kye slumped down on the bed.

That threw Ali but he could be lying. 'Why should I believe you?'

'It is what they do when they can't control you. They take someone you love away.' Kye's voice cracked.

'Who are they?' Ali asked, sick of shadows and their secrets.

'They are something that never died, they are the Descendants of Hades.' Kye admitted in a whisper.

'The Descendants are legend,' Ali scoffed but their name held a chill.

'No, they are real enough, I didn't know they would take you so soon, Yuki was not meant to be taken, but they will be back for you and they are going to use her.'

'You let this happen,' she exhaled every word, 'the poison!'

'Yes, as for the poison I had no part in that, they must have some else here. I was a nearly high guard when they took my family. They still have them to keep me in line.'

'What do they want?' Ali's mind reeling unpleasant thoughts of others out there.

'They want war.' He looked heartbroken and scared.

'When was the last time you saw your family?' she asked quietly, fear for her own family crawling in her throat. She tried to swallow the knot but she couldn't suppress it.

'After Wilvanra quit.'

'Yes, she surprised everyone, then they grabbed my family and threatened the rest to keep quiet they also grabbed others.'

'Others with the potential to be a High Guard?'

'Yes.' He looked grim.

'Do you know who they are?'

'Darshan and Marwex, one of the Lucast triplets.'

'By the gods, Alexander really does have a small army. Why wait and fight back now?'

'We were weaker than Wilvanra, we knew they had something or someone keeping her in check, they didn't get to keep you close but now they have Yuki. The attack will only push everyone's hand today, make you high guard and the council will fall because you won't stand with Atlantis. You will be a puppet for Hades.'

'We must tell the council and my family I must warn them.' Ali paced in fear.

'No, it will turn into a bloodbath and just as a small part of you still doesn't believe in any of this, a large part of the council will take it as lies.' He looked at his watch 'We must go, but hear me, we can only act while you still have freedom.'

They marched to the temple, thought the grand square was flooded with people. They moved no slower as the people parted on seeing her surrounded by shadows and guardians. They could see two councils had a stake in her claim but could they see the other force at play, a force nearly as old as time.

Ali once loved the temple but now she could feel a pressure that she never notice or how all eyes fell on her. Ali and Kye took their place and along with other guards, were the main witness of the attack.

Judge Kqean waved the glass sceptre over the room. 'We are gathered here this evening to bring a story together on the attack that took place earlier today. All evidence shall be spoken in truth.'

'Why did we not know of the attack until after it happened and we only found out when they blew the roof off?' Lunglock looked at Guardians and the Shadows.

The prison captain spoke up his face was swollen with bruises. 'They cut off the communication between us and the main island before they attacked. They gassed the first set of guards to stop them from warning the rest. We lost three guards.' The captain bowed his aching head.

Lunglock stopped another council member from speaking and held his hand for a moment of silence. Ali felt sick, innocent people had just died.

'What happened when they were in the tower?' Alexander said, taking over the questioning.

'They overpowered us,' said the prison captain, all the other guards agreed

'And you, Ali of the Redfish, what do you have to add to this story?' Alexander barked, casting disapproving eyes her way.

Ali could almost feel the heat of his temper. 'We were drugged, the doctor has confirmed it to by a sleeping poison enough for one but split between it was not enough to render us unconscious. They didn't say much, we defended ourselves and tried to escape but that was when the tower blew and we were separated.'

Just as Kye predicted, the trial ended with no one knowing who they were or what they wanted but one member did suggest they could be linked to the fallen ship because the attacker ship vanished without a trace today and someone blamed humans.

'I hear by close this hearing for today and it will reopen on new evidence gathered,' declared Judge Kqean, lifting the glass sceptre.

The doors to the temple burst open and a blizzard blew in temperature, dropped well below freezing and through the white wind walked Yuki's family.

'Where my daughter?' shouted Domariu Yuki's Father.

Lunglock stood, 'How dare you interrupt the temple with councils in session!'

'How dare you ban the family of the victim from the session and why were we the last to know of daughter's fate?' Domariu shouted back.

'You have my apologies but we are trying to find her now,' Lunglock consoled. He did sound sincere to Ali. But it was too late, the family was enraged and scared. People were dead and Yuki was taken by the unknown.

'You have lost control of this council. Atlantis is weak. I will no longer hold loyal to this council,' spat Domariu and took off the ring of this third finger on his left hand. A blue metal, a symbol of the sea surrounding Atlantis marking the Frostnar wearer bound in service.

Domariu threw the ring down at the steps of the council, Yuki's mother Narmu and her brothers cast their rings down too. Other members of the family and Frostnar culture also removed their rings. It rained rings on the temple floor, Yuki family turned on their heels and left.

'You turn your back on Atlantis when we are most in need,' Lunglock called out after them.

Domariu stopped but did not turn. 'No, I turn my back on you.'

Though they left, the temperature did not rise. Ali knew through Yuki that removing a ring was major and that a ring had not been cast down in the temple for a hundred years.

'We are in need of a High Guard even if untested,' Lunglock addressed the council crisply, reigning in his composure, which Ali thought was impressive when the mood in the temple was as frigid as the air.

'Stand if in favour of Ali Redfish.'

Ali stepped back in shock, they were doing this now with Yuki taken, a ruined tower on their flank and the floor was covered with Frostnar rings.

Lunglock sat down while everyone, including the shadows and the Line, stood. Ali looked to Lunglock, he tried to save her from this, maybe he knows about the Descendants or maybe he is one of them. Ali knew one thing, there would be war. Everyone standing looked to her, Lunglock's gaze fixed on the open temple door, Ali turned to see what he saw, the sea and setting sun. She had freedom until sunrise.

Chapter 16
Sister

'The ceremony is at dawn tomorrow and you are meant to spend tonight in the temple praying to the gods to guide you. We can get Yuki back tonight,' whispered Kye.

'Why should I trust you not to leave me there as a trade?' Ali rebuked.

'Thought you might say that so I invited your team, now you will outnumber me and besides, we are going to need all the help we can get. They keep everyone on a ship, moving so no one ever knows where they are, but the stealth ship they used today needs a lot of energy. A short-range vessel means the main ship can't be that far off Atlantis.'

'How are we going to get off Atlantis and find this ship?' Ali asked, still unsure of this plan.

'That the tricky part, we can't use Alexander's and my team will rat me out, the Descendants are watching us and we can't involve shadows we don't know.'

'Only a team knows the name of the ship and how to operate it,' Ali asked, wondering how that was at a good thing.

'Yes, security shadows only keep all missions to themselves, only high shadows see the full picture. Which is a shame because shadow ships are the fastest and likely would have got us closer to that ship without raising too much suspicion.'

'What about the Redfish?' Ali offered. That was one ship she felt she could try to fly from sitting next to Reece and listening to his chattering. It was fast, not shadow fast but the Redfish smaller than average size made her faster than other guardian ships.

Kye laughed, 'Are you crazy? They had that ship practically tied down.'

'So where are we going to get a ship then?'

'Well, I left it up to your friends.'

'You did what? We can involve them in ship stealing,' Ali stammered.

'What is the difference between stealing a ship and being on a stolen ship?' he questioned.

'They can't claim ignorance.'

'Captain Philip said he would call in some favours in at the Volt,' Kye said, defending his plan.

'The last favour in the call there ended badly and in my team being grounded.'

'You saved me and my team so no I don't think the favour was wrong, we got the ship back that started all of this,' he reasoned.

'We don't know why or how that ship went down, now we still don't have any answers but instead, we are looking for people who might be alive, the mission is different. Everyone has got to get out of there,' Ali concluded.

'No, we can't involve more people, I promise we will get them back.'

They ran to the residential island holding Yuki's family, behind the house on the shore sat an elegant and pointy black shadow ship with "Onyx Star" painted hull near the wing in sliver, smaller than the Redfish, this ship was built for speed. Yuki's family stood around it, her older three brothers in a dual dress.

They broke apart on her approach, she got hugs from Captain, Reece and Jenks. 'We missed you,' said Jenks.

'Yes, thought you were gone when the tower blew up,' Reece cringed.

'Thanks, guys,' but she couldn't smile, not with Yuki gone.

'The Dorothea sons are joining us,' Captain Philip nodded at Myron, Celeb and Kumari.

'We fight for a living, so why not fight for real,' declared Kumari.

'We are not the only ones missing someone, this is Kye. They also have taken his family,' admitted Ali, introducing him. Kye stuck hands with the brothers first, then Yuki's parents.

'Right, we best get going. We only have a short window in and out of here,' ordered the captain, climbing the ladder, Ali followed.

'How did you get the security drop in the Volt?' Ali asked.

'It wasn't the Volt, it was Lunglock, gave us the ship too, it's a training ship so it wouldn't be missed for now.' The captain explained.

Kye and Reece took their sits in the cockpit into a multicolour bubble, some dial turning and switch flicking brought the ship to life.

'How are we going to find this ship?' Ali wondered about tracking and codes.

'We are going to ask them,' said Jenks, strapping himself in beside her.

'I thought this was meant to be a sneak on and off mission.'

'They are going to find us,' said Jenks.

'Another couple of prisoners won't matter to this floating fortress, they will practically welcome us as guests, more people to hold sway over you and the Council.' Captain looked to Ali.

'So the plan is going to work because the rest of the team have left the apparent safety of Atlantis looking for Yuki and they don't know that don't know about Kye, me or the world champions in the back,' Ali surmised.

'Ya, that is basically it,' called Reece.

'What if they don't respond or we are outnumbered?' Ali probed.

'We will drop the hint that you are on board and they should come running, as for numbers, we got the Erbus in port. That is a fight no one can win,' Reece scoffed, pushing flight gears into place.

An hour out, Reece let the distress signal play and lowered the ship so they were flying just above the water, everyone turned silent. Ali began to feel more nervous, which she didn't think was possible.

'Why don't they respond, they have to know we are here,' she whispered to Jenks.

'I don't know and I don't like it much either,' sighed Jenks, 'why don't we use the messaging orb?'

'I don't think it would work, Jenks.' Captain Philip stuck his head, frowning. 'It's not like the base in a fix location, plus I wouldn't even know how to find them out here.'

'It is a game,' Reece edged. 'Both players have what the other wants. We want a location and they want us, it is a bit in between the takedown, where they will be vulnerable to attack.' He looked at the captain. 'What do you think?' he asked.

'Reece, increase the urgency and make the turn back to Atlantis,' he ordered. 'Time to see if we caught anything.'

The ship made a wide arch, dipping and rising from the water.

'Just making the ship error more obvious to them,' called Reece, the ship came straight and Reece threw in some left and right jerks.

'Alright Reece, ease up. We don't want to create any actual problems,' yelled Captain.

'Sir, a ship has just appeared on the radar, she just must be close to having made herself visible to us,' Kye guessed.

An uncomfortable thought that they were being watched the whole time swept over Ali. It was a big ocean vessel, Reece's and Kye's eyes now glued to the monitor, watching the green light dot flicker closer and closer.

'What do we do, Captain?'

'Maintain course and speed, we will attempt to make contact now,' said the captain walking to the pilot station. 'We need them close, but they are using a cloak, the flickering meaning we can't get a definite location nor can we record the radar readings, they likely have the equipment to read any outgoing messages, so we can't talk to Atlantis for now or they will vanish or take us out.'

'SOS, this is the Onyx Star, flying the Atlantis flag, we are in need of immediate assistance over.'

The radio crackled, filling the silence. The radar showed the ship hidden by darkness pulling closer began to sail parallel to us.

'This the Onyx Star, please respond. Our equipment is crashing, your ship appeared suddenly and I believe we are very close over.'

The captain gave them a beat before trying again.

'Onyx Star SOS, if you do not respond, it will be counted as a threat against Atlantis, over.'

The green stopped flickering. The radio stopped crackling, and Ali swore she could hear someone breathing.

'Acheron responding to SOS. The flight deck is being cleared, over,' a sharp voice snapped.

'Message received over.'

'Did someone just say Acheron?' said Reece, turning to look at everyone.

'A river separating our world and the underworld,' said Kye.

'Time to pay the ferryman,' said the captain. 'Bring her up Reece.'

'Scanning the ship and guns locking to theirs,' reported Kye.

'Alright Reece, you drop us and take out their guns, kye will help you from the outside. Myron, Celeb and Kumari, we are going under to find Yuki and Kye's family. Jenks you are with us too just in case anyone is injured. Ali will act as a lead distraction. As soon as we start, the game is up, Reece, you can send Atlantis a message an SOS for real.'

Reece made to land and they gathered by the landing ramp. They were high above the deck. 'I will see out here.' Ali walked out into the air and flew to the bridge tower roof at the stern, taking out their communication was vital to this mission. Landing on the roof with no one noticing, she found a grid box and began to cut wires. Below on the deck, Onyx Star landed and guards rushed to surround them. She didn't know why her power had changed but the time to question it was not now but only to use it like never before. The game was up on Ali as the ship searchlights turned on her, she flew high above the middle deck more guards poured out.

'Surrender!' a voice boomed over the ship's speaker. Ali lowered herself but as she got closer to the deck, she lifted the guards up, spinning and turning them, Ali locked their guns. The team ran for one of the open doorways Reece took to the air again. Turning to face her, she could see him smiling but it dropped as anti-aircraft guns started to take aim. Kye fired at one of the guns and it exploded. Ali dropped the guards and Reece pulled up. Bang! When the guns Bang! Bang! Bang! The air was full of smoke and Ali knew where all the missiles were aimed.

'Reece!' she screamed and reached for the ship, cloaking it, she absorbed each blast as the missile imploded on the force field. The smoke cleared and Reece was still in the air. He might be stone skin but no skin was thick enough to take missiles. Ali couldn't control her breathing. She had all this extra energy that was not hers. The guards began to shoot at her and Reece. Ali's head was filled with ringing and it felt her ears were bleeding. While the ship was to some extent, bulletproof, she was not. Bullets that reached for her erupted into light, the runes on her hands glowed. What is this? Ali couldn't surmise this new power, this was not here. Ali used the extra energy not only to shield them. She blasted the ship's guns before they could fire again.

Ali coughed shakily, her lungs still full of smoke and the volume on the ringing in her head had only decreased a notch or two. Which way was home? Ali felt the panic mixing with the smoke in her throat. Ali tried to rub the dust grains lodged under her eyelids, turning where she stood as she had up and down, but no more direction than that.

'Reece, you okay?' Ali coughed on the radio.

'By the gods! Ali, what was that?' Reece shrieked.

'I don't know, that power was not mine…can't think about it now. We got to get Yuki and back to Atlantis,' Ali coughed. *They needed to get out of here,* Ali thought, turning in the smoke.

'Up!' Ali croaked, she looked to the stars finding north. Her mother had always said, 'home was in the stars'. Ali hung on to the family in her mind while reaching for the ship engines she began to turn the ship towards Atlantis. She felt the ship fighting the pull and flew to the bridge, landing. She felt exhausted. The excess energy had been used up and she felt her own energy sapping. Ali looked down at her hand, the rune's lights fading.

The bridge was dark and cold, she expected there to be a crew and a captain yelling orders. She couldn't see Kye outside and searched the security monitors for the rest of the team. They must be controlling the ship from the engine room. 'Reece, come in,' she called over the radio. 'Reece, land on the bridge tower. This is not over and they won't fire on their own ship yet.'

Bullets rained on the glass, *well abandoned was a lie*, Ali thought, ducking down behind the wheel. 'Captain, we are not Atlantis bound. I repeat we are not Atlantis bound, the fire is still in play.' Ali tapped her chest radio but it sounded dead, it must not work inside the ship or someone was blocking them. She could hear guards running up the metal steps. She closed the door and she threw metal panelling from the walls at the windows, but she could already feel the guard's own powers acting on the simple defence. She cut all the wires from the now exposed wall cavities she could get her hands on, hoping this would hamper the enemy more than them.

Bullets started to fly through the door, not much longer until they were here. Ali crawled between the desks to a door and it opened slowly. She hoped there were no guards on the other side because the guards on this side had just broken through. Ali jumped up and ran, throwing a force field behind her. There was a deafening roar and the ship shook violently, Ali fell to the floor and so did some of the guards.

'What was that?' She heard the guards shout. She wondered too. Ali dragged herself around a corner out of the direct line of fire and clambered to her feet. She could hear guards approaching from another side. She ran for a stairwell jumping for the ladder but the ship shook again and Ali missed the ladder. She fell, luckily the roar cover the sound as she hit the metal floor groaning from the pain. The ground was so cold she almost felt stuck to it as she tried to roll away from the stairwell.

She could not go back up because the guards would be right there, she thought. Ali leaned in against the wall, cold as ice, as the guards gathered at the ladder. She moved away, her hands burning from the icy metal but the cold soothing the shoulder she landed on, numbing the pain. Ali even held her breath in case the guards saw it.

Wait, I can see my breath! Yuki! She thought and grimly was reminded of the hot and cold game, only in the opposite, the colder you are the closer you are to the finding. Ali looked right and left and realised to see there was more ice on her side of the corridor and she started to follow the ice. Two limping corridors and three painful levels lower, she came to another corridor filled with sparkling icicles growing from the floor and hanging from the ceiling.

She tapped on the door. 'Yuki, you ready to go,' she called, cracking open the door with powers, but Ali still had to physically put her back into it with an extra weight of the ice.

'What took you so long?' Yuki reprimanded, standing with her arms crossed.

'Oh, you know we got lost on the way,' Ali replied, leaning against the doorframe but the cold made acting nonchalant difficult.

Yuki laughed, 'Let's get out of here.'

The ship shook again and ice walls cracked, groaned all around them. Icicles outside came loose, smashing on the floor.

'What is that?' asked Yuki.

'I don't know and really don't want to know,' Ali said, checking their exit, rolling her injured shoulder against the door frame before stepping back in the corridor to come ice grotto.

Chapter 17
Brother

'Reece is on the bridge,' Ali whispered, taking them slowly back the way she had come, hoping the guards had moved on. Yuki was weak too, no food or drink and some of the wounds from the tower blast looked bad, bordering on infected.

One level higher, the guards found them, they ran, throwing ice and air blasts behind them, hoping to keep them at bay. They hauled themselves up to another level, breathing hard, Yuki cover well with a disc of ice. Bullets burst right through and more guards already on their level sounded. They ran down a corridor with windows and Ali could the stern of the ship. 'Out there,' she cried and they burst through a door and into the railing.

Yuki started to freeze the door shut, but Ali pulled her away.

'No time and no energy.' She pushed Yuki toward a ladder. It was a bright night as Yuki and Ali climbed the bridge tower. Ali could see the engines were still ploughing them across the sea.

'Reece, come in I got Yuki!' Ali called through the radio, hoping to the gods it worked.

'Yuki!' Reece shouted.

'We are going to the deck. The bridge tower is overrun can you get us there?' Ali pleaded.

'No! Ali, the deck is not a safe place, climb! Don't stop, I am here on the bridge roof, Gods, we are still too far from help,' Reece shouted.

'What are talking about the whole ship is not safe,' puffed Ali, climbing.

Yuki disappeared over the roof and Ali pulled herself up to see why. Reece had parked to the side, giving her and Yuki a perfect view of an ice dragon and fire dragon battling above the ship.

Reece was out of the plane running towards Yuki.

'That's Caleb,' screamed Yuki, and raced towards the dragons.

Reece caught her. 'I know, we came for you so we can all go home together,' huffed Reece, dragging her towards the plane.

'Captain, we got Yuki, let's get out of here,' the radio crackled.

'There are more people here, Reece, we can't leave,' barked the captain.

'Atlantis is too far out for this fight. We are outnumbered, Sir,' Reece calculated.

'Then we will run,' Captain Philip ordered.

'Where are you, Sir?' Reece asked, lifting the chest radio clearer.

'Bow.'

They look between the dragons and below at the front of the ship a human scale battle raged. 'We are coming to you, Captain,' Reece yelled.

'What about the dragons?' screamed Yuki. They looked closely that the ground below the dragon for their creators. Caleb stood on the starboard edge of the ship and on the port's edge stood Alexander.

'Alexander is Descendant of Hades?' Ali screeched, taking a step back in shock, another betrayal this was what Kye never told her.

'Well, this explains a lot, the ship you would need massive resources to build this thing and keep it a secret,' said Reece, hopping on the spot, nudged Yuki and Ali. 'We need to go now,' Reece called over his shoulder, running toward the ship, Yuki and Ali followed at a slower pace.

"That did explain a lot is an understatement, Reece!" Ali's mind spun. 'If the head of Atlantis security was Dark Descendant, then what about blood magic? What about the Atlantis earthquake? What about my new powers?'

'What new powers?' Yuki mumbled, her head swinging backwards to look at the fight. 'Blood magic?'

'Something has changed.' Ali chewed her lip as she glanced down at her hands 'I will tell you later.'

They jumped into the Onyx Star and Reece gave the dragons a wide berth, but Ali still sweated, hot and cold. The dragon's jaws gaped wide, showered each in fire and ice. Yuki grabbed her hand as the dragons roared. The ship shuddered but Ali couldn't tell if that was the sound waves or Reece's hand on the steering. This was no competition with simple sides. This was family against a side that never should have been possible, the secret side. Ali squeezed Yuki's hand, a humane gesture before they enter the fire.

The ship rained down on the guards, Yuki and Ali made room for the injured persons. Yuki shrieked as Myron carried Kumari on board. He had been shot in the leg. Jenks and Kye kept the guards back with fire.

While the captain used a gun and green magic that blasted through groups of guards and wrapped around individuals, hurling them as far as he could. Ali stepped off to help more people, she didn't know them for sure, but they looked like Kye's mother and sister. The next people Ali knew from only a distance. Thea Cross and Wilvanra Shadow, who was pregnant.

The dragon of fire turned on them and spreading its wings, breathed fire down upon them. Kye stopped the fire but an uncomfortable heat reached for them.

'Traitor!' roared the dragon in a voice that sounded like tearing metal. The ice dragon leap on him they twisted high into the sky, breaking apart and disappearing on the dive down.

'I challenge you to a duel!' boomed Alexander, 'your freedom if you win.'

Caleb, even from this distance, looked exhausted. A fighting brother down and the whole team was weary, yet still more guards crowded the deck. Too many to fight, their energy was running out.

'Myron, my right and Kye, my left,' said Caleb wiping the sweat from his face.

'I fight for you no more,' Kye spat at Alexander.

'I think you will. I think you always will, your family is not complete without its youngest member, is it?' Alexander laughed.

'Bjorn,' whispered Kye.

'No Kye!' yelled the captain, grabbing Kye, 'don't do it. We can get him back, we can get them all back just like we did today.' Kye's struggling slowed.

'Now, now captain don't you think Kye deserves a chance to fight for his brother, I know you would have loved the chance,' Alexander sneered.

Philips eyes glazed over his grip loosed on Kye 'Ray...the ship' Kye twisted free, while Philip's mind returned to the present 'Nooo' he roared but it was too late, Kye was running to the wrong side, Alexander waved his guards away.

'Why?' Philip pushed against the guards, they took his gun and pushed him back.

Alexander shrugged, 'It was self-defence of my life or his, of course, someone else's brother too, he laughed.' Ali hear a scream from their side and looked to see Thea holding Wilvanra.

'Who will be the second shield?' asked Myron as Caleb hugged Yuki.

Ali didn't hesitate. 'I will, I am the next in line for the High Guard.'

They stepped out in the middle of the deck, Ali on Caleb's right. 'Since you are our honoured guests, please have the first draw,' bowed Alexander.

Caleb bowed their acceptance and drew a shaking breath. Caleb flung ice dragger at Alexander, Kye melted them and Darshan threw up an electric field around them. Alexander laughed 'Is that it?' sending a fire tornado at them. Myron threw ice on the ground and Ali killed the oxygen around it.

'Let's finish this,' said Caleb grimly, sending a wave of ice down on them. Fire and electricity meet the wave in the middle of the ship. The wave was rolling back towards them with fire behind it and electricity cracking at its crest, Caleb grunted, trying to keep the wave at bay. 'Shields cannot attack us,' Ali cried.

'They're not, they are returning his attack, which we can't shield him from. He has to take what he has thrown out,' called Myron. He saw her confusion. 'It is rare but remember, it takes more energy to return than defend it.'

Two against one normal in duelling was tough but these odds were impossible, duelling experience aside these were the top Shadow Guardians. The strongest people in the world plus Kye at high guard level. These people would have never been seen in competition because there would have been no contest. Caleb was sweating even as the wall of ice was getting closer. Caleb roared and split the wall in half and ice exploded across the ship.

Alexander, clearly visible, now laughed, 'About time, my turn.' He placed a hand on the shoulders of Kye and Darshan. 'Attack with me and I will grant you one wish each.' Darshan nodded keenly, Kye seemed taken aback, but it was his brother and all he had to do was cheat the dual.

'Coward, you must be near the end of your strength to be using blackmail in a duel,' shouted Myron.

'A wish isn't blackmailing, it just giving people exactly what they want,' Alexander chuckled.

Alexander turned toward Kye, who nodded and hung his head. 'Glad we have our wishes in order.'

'And if you kill us?' Celeb called.

'Then surrender fools,' called Alexander.

Myron threw an ice shield in front of Caleb as a storm of red and white ripped across the deck towards them.

Ali started running, running towards the fire and electricity, jumping into it, screaming as she absorbed all the energy. Glowing now, she returned the attack to Alexander, his attack. 'Defend me,' shouted Alexander, 'or she will kill us all!' The three men became enfolded in fire, ice and electricity.

It took energy to take it and to give it back. 'We surrender,' cried out Darshan before Ali could get through the rest of her taken energy.

'Impossible, no one has that power,' spat Alexander.

'Captain Alexander.' An officer rushed onto the deck. 'We are not alone anymore, ships are coming from Atlantis! They have locked on to our position!' the officer's report out of breath.

'Code violet,' Alexander growled and glared at Ali, looks like some wire cutting worked after all. Guards surrounded the three men.

'Opened fire on them,' said Alexander waving a hand in their direction

Ali shielded everyone, while Alexander and his team jumped on a small ship with some guards. The rest of the guards followed suit, retreating slowly, still firing onto another ship taking to the air.

Philip wrestled a gun off a guard and started to return the fire, Jenks joined him, Reece shielded the prisoners while helping them on the Onyx Star.

'We must stop him,' shouted Caleb as they started to fly away. Ali dragged the ship back as Yuki and her brothers worked on the other firing ships, throwing ice. Caleb created the ice dragon and swatted at the ship, bringing it lower. There was so much energy being thrown around, Ali began to get confused. She began to shake and it was not only her body but the ship beneath her and in the air before her, began to shake too.

'Ali, stop! Let go of the energy,' shouted Reece.

'Ali, this is not you,' screamed Yuki.

'Ceasefire!' roared Captain Philip.

Even in his rattling airship Alexander understands the message 'Hold your fire,' Alexander shouted down and his order swept through the ranks. Ali let the energy go in light and into the sky, where storm clouds suddenly appeared. The crack of thunder cover the sound of a gun but Ali felt the bullet as it punched right through her shoulder, the force knocking her flat. From the new view on the ground, Ali could see her team and the brothers still fighting. They were slowly pulling into the ship. Yuki and Jenks were running to her, but she couldn't move and her scream held no sound.

The dragon reached for the plane with front claws as Alexander headed out of the ship with a gun Bang!

The dragon clutched its chest, rising into the sky. There was screaming on deck, Ali turning on the ground to see Caleb clutching his bloody chest. He fell to the deck as the dragon fell into the sea.

Chapter 18
Red or White

They sat in the Volt waiting for the council to open the temple, Ali couldn't cry anymore and Yuki had lost her voice too, she sat with her family. It was not a fair trade, Caleb was dead before he hit the deck. Alexander, second in command of Shadows, the leader in defence of Atlantis, was a descendant of Hades. Kye was gone, Marcus was too late and dawn was only an hour away.

'I believe you are to become the next High Guard,' said Thea, who had taken charge like she never retired or had been kidnapped.

'I think there are more important things to think about,' whispered Ali.

'This is the perfect time. It is what Atlantis needs more than ever, plus we have last High Guard to pass on the mantle,' Thea smiled at Wilvanra. Turning her strong gaze back on Ali, she said, 'You have the power.'

Ali started in her, sitting they all saw and she didn't have an explanation. Maybe she did cause the earthquake.

The doctor arrived, saving her from the talks of mantles. He wanted to check Wilvanra out too so they stepped into an antechamber for some privacy. Jenks had done a good job on her shoulder, and the doctor was pleased with Wilvanra so he returned to the rest of their party, her time for questions.

'Why did the descendants take you both?'

'I am the reason, I would not fight for them but Thea protected me as long as she could,' Wilvanra said heavily.

'When my time was up as council head, I no longer had the powers I once did, plus we knew too much about them they watched us for a long time but I knew it was only a matter of time before they killed us or brought us in. We still must be of some use to them.' said Thea, leaving Ali followed and Wilvanra.

'Where is the council?' growled Philip.

'Come on, shortcuts don't change,' said Thea, walking towards the door behind the Volt's main desk. Reece, Jenks and Ali brought up the rear, she never thought the buildings were linked. Isolated buildings for isolated purposes.

Three corridors, two secret doors and the top of a round tower later and back. They came to a side door of the temple hall. Thea knocked, 'Lunglock, it's Thea I am back' she smiled, 'that will scare him.'

'Are you sure that was a shortcut?' puffed Reece, Jenks elbowed him.

'Well, we did swing by some places where he might have been too.' she sighed and opened the door.

'Lunglock' but there was no reply, he sat slumped at a high table, wrote in a red at ran down the main wall behind him, *Lunglocked.*

'Locky!' Thea screamed, rushing up the steps to him.

'Don't touch anything,' warned Philip, drawing a gun.

Thea sobbed over Lunglock, 'Locky,' she repeated, gently pushing back his hair to feel a pulse on his neck. But she knew they all knew there was too much blood on the wall for that.

'Ali, Jenks, get Marcus now,' ordered Captain Philip.

They unbolted the main temple door and ran for the port where the Acheron docked between the Erebus and the Veracity, in under ten minutes, they were back in the temple surrounded by Shadows. Thea sat in a chair beside Lunglock and she would not be moved. A man named Justin lead a team investigator, he took blood samples and carried out tests on a lower table. Philip and Marcus whispered in a corner, while Ali, Reece and Jenks stood out of the way. None of them knew how to tell Yuki and her family. A Shadow rushed in. 'Marcus, Sir, reports in on the other council members.'

Marcus nodded, walking towards him.

'Six dead in their chambers. Others have fled into hiding. Only Esmeralda and Kqean remain in their office and are underwater. I believe that is what kept them safe.'

'Provide them with security from above,' said Marcus, turning from him 'Results!' he barked.

'He was poisoned Sir, it's a Stone skin weakness. It was a high dose of web shade, he would have suffocated as his lungs bleed and filled with blood,' said Justin, looking up from his miniature lab.

Marcus stood before Lunglock and Thea 'Red or white?' he asked.

Thea pointed to the goblet, 'Red, he trusted them.'

'The killer is one of us,' announced Marcus . 'Will you take the role as council leader back?'

'Until justice is served yes.' Thea kissed Lunglock's head. 'Rest easy, dear friend.'

'The funeral will be held at midday, bring in the Line and gather the rest of the council.' She stepped down from the table. 'Philip, a word, will your team serve me in this terrible hour?'

'That would be our greatest honour to serve you,' the captain bowed followed Recce, Jenks and herself bowed too.

'Before the council meets or what is left of it, let's meet to figure out our next steps, we must name you high guard Ali.'

There was no time to waste they stepped away from the crowd. Temple, there would be more people soon as the word of Lunglock death spread across the world.

The news was spreading quickly as the Line and the last of the council entered the temple. 'Welcome back, Thea,' said Arcwqil Dareghn.

'Will you start the preparation for the funeral?' Thea asked Arcwqil.

'Of course,' he nodded his reply.

'Do we have any prisoners?' asked Thea, turning back to Marcus.

'None,' spoke Marcus. 'The Acheron is being searched and Alexander's office here is raided as we speak but I doubt he left clues but the ship should turn up something useful and people have been returned to us, hopefully with information too.'

Wilvanra stepped from the Volt. 'Is it true?'

'Yes, but it is time for the living to step forward,' spoke Thea. 'The crossover must be now.'

Wilvanra looked past Thea. 'He couldn't even lie or pretend to side with them,' said Wilvanra.

'It was an insider, someone who knew Lunglock, who knew that he never pretend or lie,' Thea said and squeezed Wilvanra's shoulder. 'But the people need structure, we need a front line, you must reclaim place as a high guard or pass it on.'

'I will fight but I will not stand for something that is still corrupt, I can't go back,' Wilvanra announced.

'I accept that,' Thea nodded. 'Ali, the honour is yours if you would please receive the rank,' Thea spoke sombrely.

'What about my team?' Ali asked, trying not to chew a nail.

'You will not work alone,' Thea smiled, 'but the people need a champion, Atlantis needs its Guard.'

Ali took a deep breath, her family would be so proud, so worried. There was no time left to call home and tell them about a new job. 'Okay,' Ali exhaled.

Wilvanra and Ali walked alone down to the water's edge. 'I am not ready,' Ali confessed, looking at the water in shame.

'It's not about how powerful you are, not really, it is about what you do with it and who you are with power.'

They sat and undone their boots. 'What is it like being a high guard?' asked Ali, It was nice to be around someone who had seen it before.

'Lonely, you can't trust anyone except the council and then I couldn't understand what they wanted from me or why would I do the missions they sent when they were wrong. I left because if I kept saying no, I would end up being on a mission with no survivors. Thea couldn't see what they had become until it was too late, they would have got rid of her soon. But it should be different now. The secret is out.'

'Where are these council members now?'

'It was not just the innocent who fled the city.'

'How could this happen? Do they still want the same things as the legend?' Ali asked, confused.

'The Descendants have always been there. To most, only a myth but enough of them survived to be real, and they grew. They still want war with humans and the planet to themselves just like the humans think they have it all.'

'Why now? Surely there were other times better for war. Plus, why kill people on your side and no one touched the Line either,' Ali asked confused.

'They have the numbers, resources, power, that I think they would have slowly made their move in this age, but things are changing. Things are moving fast now because of an event even they didn't see coming. As for the killings, it is all for control but the Line is as old as Atlantis. They rule beside the kings once before the high council was created. To attack them is to attack the stone itself.' Wilvanra explained sombrely.

'What changed their minds?'

'The signs are here, I believe it is not the first time that it happen, the last Atlantis shook was the day it was lost to the sea.' Wilvanra said looking across the sea.

'Where will we stand in this war?' Ali could only look at her hands.

'We will stand against all wars, it how the council was born it, why Atlantis is still here.'

Ali nodded, their place here was to stop the war and find peace between people. They walked down the steps into the sea, washing away who they were ready to become, something else, a role of something more. Stepping out, Wilvanra told her the ceremony words, 'Traditional there are meant to be robes, candles and offering to the gods, but we must put that all aside for the moment.'

In the dawn light on the steps before the temple, Ali kneels before the Line and Thea. 'I will serve Atlantis and her people with my life, I will stand against all who seek to harm the present or the future at the heart of our world/' Ali repeated the words she learned from Wilvanra. There was a pause and Ali looked from Reece and Jenks, who smiled sadly at her, to Captain Philip, who nodded. Yuki and her family stood in the doorway at the right of the Volt, not quite ready to step into this new day. But neither was Ali, ready for this fight, the losses so heavy and the war had not even begun.

'Arise, Ali Redfish, High Guard of Atlantis,' said Thea.

Chapter 19
Their Place

'Should we not be getting ready for a war?' Reece asked aloud, the inaction making him itch. Fight mode still turned on from their last skirmish, Ali knew how he felt. She didn't remember the last time she slept well or easily. She didn't know what the team or herself were running on anymore 'orders' popped into her mind. *Whose orders?* She cast the thought aside. Thea was on the right side and Lunglock knew what was going to happen. In the end, he helped them get this far to expose them just before they exposed themselves.

'No dear, it is time to grieve,' Thea said softly from the doorway of the temple and down the steps, out of the side they bring out Lunglock's body.

'But they could attack again,' Jenks spoke out a mood linked to Reece's.

'They have already cleared the battlefield, don't you see killing Lunglock and his supporters before the fighting became open before they decided to step into the light, also showing people the fall of their leaders,' Thea explained 'We lost this battle.'

'But we will be vulnerable in grief,' Reece retorted.

'Grief makes you mortal,' she sighed heavy. 'Ancient Atlantis tradition marks burial outside of wartime.' Thea looked up to the tower of the temple, the rising sun making the white stone glow.

A silence befell the group, as they knew someone would leave the temple for the last time. Thea, Captain Marcus, Kqean and Esmeralda lead the procession followed by two infirmary staff carrying a stretcher with a sheet over it. Ali and the team heads hanging but they were not alone. She turned to the square to see it had filled with silent people and the water beyond was filling with small boats carrying more people closer. The sky above them hummed with airships coming into land on the already crowing islands. The word had spread and people were not fleeing, they were returning. They knew what happen here at the heart would affect the whole world.

Thea, seeing the gathering crowd, moved down a step to stand with them. 'Today we bury our dead and ask the questions we already know the answers to. Tomorrow we will stand for those who could not stand anymore.' There was sorrow in that voice but it rang clear as a bell thought the square.

The group carried on, walked the short way to the Volt slowly and respectfully. There was no denying who they carried.

Thea stopped by them once more. 'Get some rest before the ceremony, it will be after midday, I must go now and oversee the operations.' Thea beseeched them before leaving for the Volt.

Many looks were thrown their way and Ali wished they weren't so high, giving people a good view. Samar bounded up the steps to them, 'Ali, if the dorms are too crowded, you and your team are welcome to stay in the library.'

'Thank you, that would be wonderful,' she tried to smile but found she couldn't, so she turned away to find her gaze landing on the Volts' closing doors.

'We will send a message for Yuki to let her know where you all are,' said Samar quietly.

Ali could only nod, this was all too much and all too horrible for words. They followed Samar back to the library. Ali bumped into Reece as the crowd gently jostled, breaking up to find their own spaces. They linked arms, small comfort to know someone else had the same day and night as you.

They entered the calm of the library and Ali felt cold and more tired than she ever felt in her life, funny how doorways make you suddenly aware of your mental or physical state. Samdar coughed from behind them, looks like he got caught in the crowd.

'He will be missed, they all will be missed,' he coughed he offered the old salute to them. Samdar had lost a dear friend but he didn't quite believe it yet. Samar leads them upstairs to the rooms. Ali looked back to see Samdar shuffling over to the desk, the great hulking piece looked sturdy and resilient.

The sheets were cold and smelled fresh, they must have been just changed for them. Ali felt grateful drifting off to sleep. Too exhausted, Reece didn't bother with a Babylon Lantern climbing into the bunk above Jenks. Gentle tapping on the door woke them and Ali felt like she just closed her eyes but she could see the sun peeking through the window blind they must have got a few hours, something to keep them standing. But they had to face something more, sometimes what comes after a battle is harder than the battle itself.

Ali rose and slowly went to the door, Maizann stood on the other side. 'A late breakfast?' her smile was hopeful.

'Sounds good.' Ali couldn't refuse. They needed to eat anyway but it almost seemed like a chore.

'How is the injury?' Ali inquired.

'Healing well, thank you, but there will be a scar. So much for friendly fire,' she laughed. She seemed to think her crazy and tried to rein on her laugh. Ali smiled at her and they giggled for a moment at the craziness of it all but maybe none of it was really funny, but maybe they couldn't cry for the moment.

'Heard you got shot,' said Maizann sobering.

'Not friendly fire,' Ali edged, rolling her stiff shoulder. The same shoulder she landed on too but it felt better, better than it should, maybe it was the extra energy.

Maizann led them through the living area and Ali could see Cressida, Dominic, Linn, Drusilla, Cornelia and Zack sitting at a low table drinking tea on a large balcony facing the sea.

'I made extra porridge and there is fruit and bread as well,' said Maizann. 'You know where everything is still?'

Ali laughed, 'Yes, if guys haven't moved any around.' Ali took bowls and cutlery from a deep drawer.

'I will just leave this here,' said Maizann, laying a pot of tea in the middle of the kitchen table. She left them to themselves and joined the others outside.

Jenks glanced at his watch. 'An hour to go,' he sighed. 'What does one wear to a state funeral anyway?' he wondered bits of bread and porridge.

'Our uniforms, if we can find clean ones, I think?' but Ali was not sure there hadn't been any state funerals in a long time, not since she was a kid. 'You both should meet the rest of the scholars here.'

'Oh ya, let's meet your other team,' Reece smiled, 'anyway I think I recognise one or two from my days of study.' They stepped out onto the balcony, a beautiful sunny day without a breeze but Ali could feel a power surrounding them she looked to Cressida and smiled, she was keeping the wind out. Ali made the introductions and they talked about happier things and times. Ali moved to the edge, looking out over the sea and outer islands, which were receiving more ships both from the air and water.

Cressida joined her squeezing her hand. 'Don't forget strength is not just for the battles it is also needed for everyday life,' and she let the shield drop and wind wrapped around them the cries of alarm and someone spilled their tea 'Cressida, we are getting cold,' called Drusilla.

'You got to look after yourself too,' and the wind dropped. 'Congratulations on the promotion,' she smiled.

Ali bumped into her. 'You do that all the time,' Cressida laughed. 'It is refreshing.' Ali did not feel fresh at all just now. The sweat and grime made her want to itch.

'Thanks, Cressida' Ali smiled but with sleep and food taken care of, Ali needed to get ready for something she could never be ready for.

After showering and hunting down clean uniforms, they left for the Volt. Ali, Reece and Jenks stood with Thea and the last of the council. Yuki stood to the side with her family. They all stood in the doorway of the Volt as the Line stepped out of the temple, they would lead the ceremony as was traditional.

'The Line are all still here,' Thea said, nodding sadly in their direction.

'But they must have known it was happening,' Recce mumbled.

'Some are too old to run or because they have seen it before when they were children, they would have seen wars of unbelievable cruelty, carnage and horror,' Thea murmured from the side of her mouth. 'Open warfare does not happen overnight.'

All this fighting had happened in the shadows but burring the dead in the light of day. There was no hiding from the truth and the airship crash was no accident. The square all cleared to the edges and the steps and docks filled with people. Those who could not stand on land, stood in boats and on the bridges and islands. Lunglock, Ray, Caleb and the other fallen were carried to the centre of the square. Nineteen coffins were laid out Captain Phillip, Myron and Kumari helped to carry them.

The Line sang deeply voices silencing the wind. They sing for peace and for harmony, for those dead and for those that lived. The gathered crowd wept openly now. Ali had been so close to the fighting she forgot everyone who had no idea legends were coming alive but this story, this reality was no less frightening. The song developed chanting undertones, the air began to fill with magic. Rising out of the sea in the east came a wooden and stone longboat covered in coral. It slowly flowed through the air above the people and came to rest on the ground beside the coffins in the middle of the square. The Line turned west to face the temple, raising their hands the temple spire split and cracked right down the middle and parted creating a shining stone portal. The coffins were lifted into the boat. The crowd murmured and chanting mixed with crying too, this would be the last time these fallen people were present as they passed through the split spire, they would become stone and part of Atlantis forever.

The boat rose into the air and slowly sailed through the portal in the sky. The boat continued toward the dead island. On the buried island of Atlantis, only the dead went to the island. At sunset, the boat would return to the east and the portal would close after it.

Ray and his team were buried with full Atlantis honours alongside Lunglock and the six fall council members. Guardians and shadows who had to fall into the attack. Ali couldn't take her eyes off the sixth coffin unmark. Who was this a guest on the ship, a prisoner?

Thea Cross words replaced the dying chanting. Arms open and weeping, she shared her own grief with everyone openly. 'The enemy is not standing across from us on the battlefield, no, they are standing beside us. And in some cases, the enemy is within us. Our own doubts and fears tell us to give up on our dream to cast them aside, to stay still, to back into the shadows, well, I tell you now is not the time to step back but the time to step forward, to turn the lights on. Here we know death, we know ourselves and we will know our enemy.'

Chapter 20

The Ship of the Dead

Part of the new job Ali did not expect was that she had to watch over the dead and the death ship passage back east. Wilvanra stood with her on her first watch, one that she never should have taken. The sun was setting behind the island. As it sunk the lower the ship began to rise. The Line stood on the steps of the temple, blessing the return. As the sun finally disappeared, the ship passed through the portal, which lit a beam of light into the night sky. Once the ship passed, the light beam dropped as the portal began to close. The ship sank into it, resting beneath the stars and beneath the waves.

But she was not alone with Thea and her remaining council, the Line, her team and Marcus joined her.

'I remember my first watch,' coughed Wilvanra, 'and I hoped I would never have to watch over that ship today.'

'Who was the sixth?'

'My friend,' said Wilvanra

'I am sorry to hear that.'

'We all lost someone but Julius was not only mine to lose, he was Marcus' older brother. I will let in on my secrets, it may keep you safe.' Wilvanra kept her eyes on the ship, while Ali's eyes flicked to Marcus. It was not long ago she remembered him saying to Philip that he was not the only one to lose someone. He gave nothing away, like one of the statues in the temple.

'Why do you say that?'

'Not here. There are others looking for this truth too and only some deserve to hear it. If the truth was let loose now, it could put everyone in danger.'

'All of this for a power struggle,' Ali whispered.

'It is more than that Ali, it is for love and in the end, it was for life or death,' said Wilvanra quietly. 'I must speak with Marcus. I will see you in the temple soon.' Everyone must have seen Wilvanra's departure for her as a sign of the ceremony at an end and they slowly turned to leave too. Yuki had Rex, who was stuck to her like glue, maybe he was afraid she might leave again. They hugged and didn't say anything but just watched the waves for a while.

'Now, I know why the oracle told me to go home because it was the last time we would be a whole family.'

Ali didn't know what to say, she only hoped that this time would never come for them again. If the oracle was right about Yuki needing time, what about history repeating itself? Ali felt cursed and that she had cursed them all now. There was more truth to this story to be told. 'Can you come with me to the temple?' Ali asked Yuki.

Ali and Yuki, with Rex, said goodnight to the rest of their team and followed Wilvanra to the temple. Moments later, they stood before a guard who knocked on antechamber door for them.

'Madame Wilvanra, Yuki Redfish and the High Guard for you,' the guard called through the cracked door.

'Come in,' yelled Thea.

Thea didn't take her eyes from her paperwork 'Take seats, please,' and continued muttering to herself, 'I hope the ship returned well?'

'Yes,' said Ali, who was trying to make herself comfortable, which was not easy. She just felt inadequate plus she only got the job this morning.

'Thea,' Wilvanra broke the silence, 'I am ready.'

Thea Cross dropped her papers and looked up, she only nodded.

'I kept it to myself to protect everyone, what they don't know can't hurt them.' She turned to look out the small window. 'I joined the shadows straight out of college, placement on the Veracity. I was working on the Veracity for a few years when the job of a High Guard became free, Captain Artemis put my name forward. I was not the only one being offered. Captain Alexander put himself forward. The high council laughed at him, saying he could only have one job or the other so he decided to remain shadow captain here on Atlantis. It was not long after I took the job that things started to go bad on this part, you know but what you don't know is my parents were kidnapped and marriage was offered.'

'Of course, it couldn't be Alexander. The marriage had to be someone high up in the Descendants but not in the public eye, and a marriage like that would only bring you more power in the circle. My husband to be would become second in command. His family can be traced back to the first Descendants. Days after the proposal, Alexander learned something about me no one else knew, I suppose I would not have been able to hide it for long.' She rested her hand on her stomach. 'Because the only man I loved was Julius's brother Marcus.'

'Alexander thought the truth would tear the brothers apart and give him all their power, but Julius and I did not love each other. More than that, Julius and I broke command by refusing to marry each other.'

'I couldn't keep saying no to more missions so I retired, Alexander blackmailed us all for a while so Julius tried to help me go into hiding. Of course, Alexander found us and he wanted to teach us a lesson, we split up and ran. Ray's ship was carrying Julius to Atlantis. He wanted to expose Alexander not to Atlantis court but to the Descendants. I knocked on Thea's door and I am so sorry Thea. That night we were both kidnapped and Ray's ship was shot down.'

'The Descendants are here on Atlantis?' Yuki's jaw dropped.

'Yes, and I am not sure how much of this story they know and if Alexander is acting under their orders or his now.'

'Marcus told us he was not the only one to have lost the day the ship was brought up, he knew his brother was on board,' Ali said, thinking to the deck of the Erebus.

'Do you know who the Master Descendant is?' Ali asked.

'No, I was not trusted, Julius believed but he also loved his family, I think for most of his life they were the same thing. The descendants are bound to each other and they swear to the god Hades to keep their secrets. They are fighting to control Atlantis. Ali, they will use you or kill you not just for their cause but the Descendant war among themselves now and they will never share your power.'

'A power struggle and feud with the ranks this more than we could have hoped for, a weakness to our advantage which at the moment, we are going to need all the advantages we can get,' sighed Thea sitting back in her chair.

'Which side will Marcus choose?'

'Marcus always knew the crash was not an accident, but to know the murderer was from his people it has shaken him. It is his right to ask for blood from the Descendants, but it is the master who will decide if it will be granted, which means the master must decide who their favourite piece is, who the most powerful and useful in this war ahead.'

'Has he asked for the blood yet?' wonders Ali.

'I don't know. He refuses to talk about any of it now. I think he must not be seen to choose or he will be lost. Those sides will, the descendants and Atlantis,' Wilvanra explained. 'But know this, he also believes in the republic.'

'This is our chance if we give Marcus the chance not of revenge and blood but for justice which is owned to us more than just Marcus's family,' Thea looked to Yuki, 'and her family and Philip's family and many others too.' Thea cast her papers aside. 'We should not be preparing for war but for court.'

Chapter 21
Statues

The death of Lunglock and council members shook their world. The truth about the crash and those responsible spreads like wildfire. The fear that a legend had been growing among them broke the mirage of calm and control. Who was really in control? Ali couldn't fandom at it, maybe the Descendants had been in control for a long time. There were more riots in the hidden cities, even some protesters taking the side of the Descendants. Thea was trying to move quickly to fight the panic before it set in and took over completely.

The court, or what was lcft of it, was assembled in the temple. The empty seats starkly betrayed the dead and deceiving. Thea had invited their half of the world to join them. She send the word out that the trial was for everyone because it was their future in the balance. Atlantis rule or Descendant rule, which would lead to war against the humans.

There was no room in the temple and still, people were trying to push in, the air was heating up and so were people's tempers. Ali stood behind the high table, 'Thea,' she called, there was no point in whispering as she would not be heard. 'This is getting out of hand.'

'Stop! Everyone out now!' ordered Thea, 'we will restart the trial outside.' There was a cheer from the back of the crowd, clearly an uncomfortable spot to be in. Then suddenly the temple drained as people began to push their way out.

'Thea, this is unheard of the walls of the temple uphold our laws,' barked Arcwqil Dareghn.

'This temple has been shaken, times are changing and we must change with them. Everyone has the right to decide their own fate.'

'May the fates allow it to be,' Arcwqil nodded, leading the Line out of the temple.

Ali was blinded by the sun stepping out but she knew the square was full as the sound hit her like a physical force. She was joined by her team, standing on a step above the crowd for the vantage point. The councillors Kqean, Esmeralda, Wilvanra and Marcus flanked Thea at the top step. The Line stood behind them, not quite ready to give up their temple's walls.

'A plane went down over the Southern Ocean. We lost a great guardian team. But they were not alone in the skies that day nor were they alone on aboard, they carried a secret. A secret that could reawaken history. This secret is carried by few but each has the power to release the secret.' Thea lay the tale before the people but Ali began to feel sick. Thea's words echoed an oracle.

'The sixth person on the ship, secret bearer, the man whose life was secret, was Julius Shadow and he was a Descendant of Hades.' there were shouts of fear and disbelieve. People didn't want to believe in the rumours but these rumours were alive, strong and healthy. Ali thought of Alexander, a pillar of Atlantis but really he was tearing it down. He was setting the stage for the Descendants.

'Being a member of this group is not against our laws but it was a member of this group who shot down the ship. The Descendant's fought humans long ago and when that fight ended, it was as though they did too. Julius Shadow wanted to be free and he wanted to free others and expose the Descendant for laws they had started to break,' Thea continued, 'today we are here for justice and the right to choose our future. We will not go to war! Not among ourselves! Not with humans! But that does not mean we will not stand and fight for what is right!' the crowd cheered.

'Today we put the Descendants of Hades on trial for kidnap, hostage keeping, blackmail and murder.'

'Alexander and his team are members born to Descendants or cast into, other members include councillors, guardians and civilians. The groups are declared condemned by this court and the person involved will face justice.'

'Tomorrow will be a day of evidence against the Descendants.' Thea bowed to the crowd and returned to the temple.

Since they had captured no one and no one else was admitting to being a member, the trial ended. They couldn't expose Marcus as he had no involvement with the murders and in the end, he was being blackmailed and Ali had a terrible feeling that it was not over. No one said anything to him, the secret was out on who he was but no one could touch him for those same reasons. He was an important piece to both sides, either could give him up or stand against him, fearing the other side would join the attack.

*

'The garden islands are producing as much food as they can but we will need more to support this many people and if war comes, we will need even more,' said councillor Kqean.

'Speak with Marcus and Captain Artemis about their supplies and we will have guardian ships start flying the supply lines. I will start going through the evidence from the Acheron. They must have left some clues. This is not just chaos, this is organised and a group or a body as a head,' said Thea. Councillor Kqean headed towards the docks while her team and the Line retreated to go through the enemy's paperwork.

They sifted through papers for hours until it grew dark outside. Onboard communication was uncoded and names of ex-councillors, guardians and duellers were recognised. Both inside cells and outside of the cell. All off-board ship communication was coded and they had no luck in cracking it.

'We need someone from the inside even just to give us a piece of the code,' said Philip.

'Even if we had captured someone, they could change the code every day so it would be no good,' said Jenks. 'What about Captain Hayden or Artemis?'

'Captain Hayden, Alexander and Artemis are loyal to Marcus,' said Wilvanra.

'Unless they remained on the inside,' said Philip, looking at Thea.

'Marcus will never talk. He stands still between us, I think he kept a balance over the years,' said Thea.

'Then the only other person who turned for us turned back,' said Philip. No one spoke his name.

'What about the prisoners?' asked Reece. 'They must have a connection with the Descendants.'

'That would be useful,' agreed Thea. 'So far, the only reason Wilvanra and I were taken was to keep Marcus in check and Yuki was taken because of Ali, but we learned nothing from our cells. Any luck with the others recused from the Acheron?'

'No, nothing so far. We interviewed them when they first came in,' said Arcwqil. 'We will try again tomorrow. Maybe something will come back to them. There are some requesting permission to return home.'

'It is still not safe. They were taken for a reason. Have any more agreed to speak on the trail tomorrow?' Thea questioned.

'No, and many have backed out, now too scared,' sighed Arcwqil.

'Marcus is the only live link we have got who hasn't tried to kill us. Why can't we force him to talk?' growled Philip.

'Because Alexander and Marcus are battling their own war in order to see who will be next, the leader. On the outside, we see these two men have all the power, but someone is higher than them. Someone is keeping them in check but their time is coming to an end, so things are accelerating. The councillors killed were on Lunglock's side, those who fled did the killing,' said Wilvanra. 'Lunglock knew something of Descendants, he knew of the struggle between Alexander and Marcus, he knew they would crown a new king of Atlantis. When Alexander held Thea and me, he had power over Marcus but Lunglock would never allow the republic to be broken.'

'There hasn't been a king since Atlantis drowned,' laughed Philip. 'This is impossible.'

'The high council is gone, we have no more power except those in this room and the faith of the people outside, but everyone else is picking a side,' said Thea.

'How did they get away with funding an operation of this scale?' asked Yuki, standing and looking closer at a picture of the Acheron, its detailed blueprint hung on the wall.

'Some of the people being held hostage were paying the Descendant or their families were giving them money,' explained Arcwqil.

'It's more than that some of the councillors who fled had been funnelling money away from Atlantis for years,' said Esmeralda. 'Councillor Kqean and I were in the Volts today, going through treasury archives and linking back to councillor offices here.'

There was so much undermining within Atlantis, no wonder it fell. It was an inside job, Ali thought.

'Alright, enough for tonight we need to be ready for tomorrow, the trail will restart tomorrow at midday,' declared Thea bringing their session to an end.

They all slept on cots in the antechamber to Thea's office. The other councillors, all took up offices in the same tower as not to spread guards thin and cover a bigger area. Ali was the first to take watch walking around the temple. She met other guards on their own patrols. Atlantis and its people had spoken today. They had told the world where they stood; *it was now the turn of the Descendants*, Ali thought. She feared their next move but she also hated the waiting, this silence across no-man's-land. Expect they didn't even know where no-man's-land was and the battle for the heart city had begun. They had also taken the fight to them too when they boarded the Acheron. They had lost so many people already, and Ali didn't want to lose anymore.

She stopped in the great hall and looked to the back. Even though the blood had to be cleaned away, Ali swore she could still see the letters but she knew it was only her imagination. She walked around the cold marble statues of the gods and kings. The only king not standing was the last but his image was carved into the back wall. To serve as a reminder to those who serve Atlantis. A price will be paid for power. Lunglock was not trying to be king, he was trying to protect the people and the last of the city. Ali wondered among the statues was it the gods who cursed Atlantis or man.

On returning to her cot, she woke Jenks for his shift. She could see the captain's Babylon lantern was dark, so much had happened she was not surprised he was awake. But sleep was like escape until you woke up. Ali needed that escape now just to shut her eyes against it all just for a moment.

'There has been an attack on the library,' said Philip shaking them all awake.

'Jenks and 1 will stay with Thea and bring in the backup, rest of you get over there now,' Philip said throwing bulletproof vests at them.

Chapter 22
Portal

They raced across the square dawn, lighting their way through the mist, but Ali could smell the smoke was mixing with mist. The great library doors, blackened and twisted by fire, still smouldered.

Samdar laying on the floor, Samar holding him as the scribes gathered around. Cornelia acting as a med officer. 'He is okay just unconscious, he will have to go to the infirmary just to be on the safe,' Cornelia assured.

'Who did is this?' Yuki gasped.

'Did Samdar say who did this?' Reece questioned.

'No, he just said, forgive me, old friend.'

'Scrolls and orbs are missing,' reported Cressida.

'Which level?' Asked Ali.

'Level 5.'

Ali and Yuki looked at each other, the twin orbs, a question and answer, a cure and a curse. 'Alexander wanted this library clear before he fled, what if he came back?' wondered Ali aloud.

'That's not possible. This island is heavily guarded,' Reece coughed, taken aback in disbelieve.

'Alexander used to be head of security on this island, he would have known if there were weaknesses or he could have created them himself when he was here,' argued Ali.

'Marcus and Artemis are here,' Reece interjected.

'Marcus is a Descendant,' Ali whispered.

'What if it was one of them, then the orbs still could be on the island,' supplied Yuki.

'Great, then we are all on the same Island as a Descendant of Hades,' Reece groaned, throwing his arms in the air.

'We have to find that orb, it could be a weapon, something we don't have, or another curse,' Ali spoke rapidly, her mind racing, was this it? Is history repeating itself? The last Atlantis was at war within itself when a curse was released.

'Did anyone see anybody leaving after the attack?' asked Reece.

'No, we just heard loud noises and came running, but it was too late,' Samar spat furiously. The doors of the library moaned farther open and everyone was ready in defensive positions but it was just the infirmary staff coming for Samdar. 'I will stay will him, Cressida. You're in charge then.' Samar fury faded to fear for his papa.

'Why was he alone?' asked Reece.

By the drowned king, nowhere is safe, not even the library, Ali thought miserably. Ali looked around the great hall. This place held stories of battles and betrayal, the library was not meant to host them literally. Ali paced the hall hoping to come across a clue but if the Descendants hid for hundreds of years, it was doubtful they left something now. Still, Ali needed to look if only to make this scene before her real and to feel useful. The only trace was the smell of charred wood, which made her nose tingle.

'We were taking turns patrolling, he guessed that they would be back,' said Cressida. 'He was right.'

'The chances of finding this person are slim unless they want to be found. Then it was a trap, they have been hiding all this time and that could have been for years.' Yuki formulated, worried biting her lip.

'What are we going to do?' asked Maizann.

The question was met with silence. Still, Ali thought, *it was nice to know that they were in this together, together in the unknown*. Suddenly an idea bloomed, Ali turned back to the group. 'We need to find out more about the descendants and about twin orbs.'

'You want to sit down and study when we are being attacked by an ancient creed?' Reece choked.

'Well, someone has to go back and tell Thea and Philip what just happen,' Yuki suggested offering Reece another deal.

'I'll be back. Just watch out for paper cuts,' Reece called out as he left.

'You've got books on twin orbs and the Descendant, right?' asked Ali.

'We will find something but I think most of the Descendants books are in the children section,' said Cressida.

159

'What are they doing there?' asked Yuki, taken aback.

'They were a myth, a fairy tale,' Cressida shrugged.

They all headed up the first floor, where a great table overlooked the main door, *a good vantage point as well*, thought Ali. Everyone split up to find books and scrolls. Ali worry as she browsed the shelves. Was this the right thing to be doing? Should they be doubling the defences? She could hear the wind whistling through the gaps in the main door. It didn't shut properly anymore. Cornelia and Zack returned with pots of tea and a cup for everyone. Dominic rolled over a blackboard on wheels to the end of the table with hesitant glances 'It is for the bigger picture,' he declared.

Ali was surprised when they managed to cover the table with books and scrolls. A good thing they had material, but she hoped they now had the time to get through it and that it was really worth it.

Dominic split the blackboard in half, writing on one side "twin orbs" and on the other side "Descendants". He then threw a piece of chalk at Drusilla 'Your side' and sat opposite her.

'Right side, we all know some of these stories from growing up with them ourselves, so we have a basic history but if you find anything different or new, we can add it to the Descendant side,' said Cressida.

'The Descendants were worshippers of Hades, the god of the underworld,' said Linn, flicking through a children's book.

'They were around before the fall of Atlantis,' said Linn. 'This history book says they all died when Atlantis drown but the stories my Grandfather told me are different. He said they lived.'

'So far we have who and from when we know that your grandfather's stories and the other are true because they are here with us today,' said Drusilla, writing. They were all silent for a while and Ali thought, she just still couldn't believe they were talking about the Descendants and the fact they still didn't know any more about them.

'What about the twin orbs?' asked Yuki.

'It is hard to say,' answered Cressida. 'There is a master list describing all the twin orbs and what they contain. They crop up in stories and actual history but many were made in secret because that was their point for keeping secrets. Plus, like real twins, they don't have to look identical.'

'We know that the Descendant wants to rule solely and the only way is to take control of humans, which means breaking the curse. The orb must give them more power or break the curse itself,' said Yuki. 'The two must be connected.'

'We have a whole section on the fall and curse,' said Cressida. 'Did anyone bring anything like that?' there were mumbled no's as everyone rose to collect more material.

'I brought help,' called Reece, pushing through the main door. Ali looked down over the balcony to see accompanied by Philip, Jenks, Thea, Wilvanra and Esmeralda.

'I will get more tea,' said Zack.

The table was fully surrounded and covered in sacks of books and scrolls but the blackboard was still mostly blank.

'Why to wait until now to take the orb,' asked Jenks.

'This is not the first time people have tried to remove material from the library, only this time they succeeded,' said Maizann. 'Alexander tried to take material from the library before he left.'

'But it couldn't have been him,' objected Reece, 'and why wait? They must have known about this orb before it came here.'

'The library is the safest place in the world for orbs, and apparently, it was also not just in safekeeping but close to hand. Only they just couldn't collect it when they came in when Captain Hayden came looking to take out books permanently,' said Cressida.

'If it the safest place in the world, how did they get in?' asked Philip.

Ali could see it on people's faces, was Samdar a Descendant? But no one dared to say it out aloud.

'What if Samdar knew them?' wondered Thea.

'A strange time to go and visit the library,' said Reece.

Wilvanra spoke up for the first time there, 'I think Thea is right, Samdar must have known them to let them in.' she stood and turned to the entrance to them. 'But I think they let themselves out.'

Ali looked closer that the doors and realised they were bent out, not in. Samdar either changed his mind about letting the orb go or he changed his mind after letting them in.

'The orb is either key to breaking the curse or is power giving. One way or another, the curse is going to be broken soon,' said Thea.

'But Atlantis is split between those who want power over humans and those who want peace. The Descendants need more power that is why they have infiltrated the high council, why they wanted Ali, me and so many others. They are looking for more power because they need it, we could destroy each other but together we are most powerful. Atlantis would become the centre of the world again,' said Wilvanra. 'The orb is the key to their power because they know the curse will be broken.'

Shouts rang around the table. The impossible can't be possible. 'The curse is forever', 'the caster is dead so it can't be broken', 'every way has been tried', 'it is the gods who have willed it so'.

Thea banged the table with a book and everyone became quiet. 'The Descendant has just accepted something we have not yet, it is giving them more power, they believe the impossible is possible.'

'I think we can all agree that Atlantis shaking was the first sign that the curse could give way,' said Esmeralda glancing at Ali. 'The whole of Atlantis shook not here on the surface but my people below said the rest of the new city shook too.'

Ali remembered the arch cracking and the pain, but not much else.

Dominic flipped the blackboard and wrote 'curse breaking' at the top 'any ideas'. Drusilla spread her arms wide over the table indicating all the books, 'Just what has not worked over millenniums?'

'Going on the presumption that we still don't have power over the curse. I think we should concentrate on what we can do if the descendants gain more,' Thea said. 'They must have other twin or they don't want us to use one.'

Cressida confirms the suspicion, 'We only had the one half and no records of the other.'

'What kind of power could the orb give them?' asked Philip.

'Anything from a new weapon, it could be the secret to the ancient power that was held by Atlanteans or to another curse. Samdar was doing research on the orb and the only thing he wrote about the orb is that it's old and it was made here in the city and we have no record of it ever being back until now,' said Cressida.

Chapter 23
The Trailing Hour

Ali and the team escorted the councillors back to the temple for the trail at midday, which was almost upon them. The square had started to fill with people again, ready to hear the stories of others who had close encounters with the Descendants. Ali thought, *they needed some real proof and maybe some were hoping it was all just a mistake.* Councillor Kqean handed Thea the echoer's potion.

'We won't have a trial, all the prisoners they are refusing to give evidence,' declared Arcwqil, joining them on the temple steps.

'I will stand,' uttered Yuki, her voice wavering. Everyone turned to look at her.

Wilvanra hugged her, 'Thank you.'

'Welcome all to who have joined us to hear the truth, to hear the stories and trial the Descendant has had a hand in weaving.' Thea's voice rang through the square.

'Atlantis was attacked days ago by people we now know to be the Descendants,' Thea said, pointing to the destroyed tower. 'Baron Lunglock and the high council members Onlex, Salnari, and Caleb were murdered the very night the Acheron was overthrown. Councillors Worlan, Samgy and Rosalind are believed to be involved and there is more evidence that they are not the only crimes these council members committed. Council member Rosalind is unaccounted for, we believe she fled Atlantis, either she is a part of the Descendants or in fear. Evidence of more personal account,' Thea coughed to clear her throat. 'I myself was taken months ago and kept against my will, my family were forced to keep quiet for my safety.' Thea stood to the side and let Wilvanra step forward to speak.

'I, Wilvanra Shadow, the last High Guard, was taken because I would not side with the Descendants, I was also told to keep my family in check.'

'I am Yuki of the Redfish, I was taken by the Descendants and kept on the Acheron. My family and friends came to recuse me but they found others like me and recused them too. My brother Caleb...' Yuki paused, looking for her family in the crowd, crying now she had found them 'Celeb was murdered by Alexander Shadow, captain of Atlantis.'

Shock rippled through the crowd. Alexander was meant to protect them and the last defence of the island. Thea let their words sink in before speaking 'Alexander did not act alone. Many Descendants stand with him, but we do not stand-alone either. We will have justice and we will have freedom again.'

'Freedom!' the crowd roared back.

Marcus appeared from the crowd and climbed the steps towards them. 'Are you going to give evidence?' asked Thea.

'I have something better,' Marcus replied, taking the stage beside her to then turning to the crowd he roared, 'I want blood!'

The words filled the square and Ali dreadfully realised he was talking to the master Descendant, they were here in the crowd.

'Nooo!' shouted Wilvanra but the words had been spoken. Ali shivered at the silence that followed.

'By the gods, get everyone off the island,' said Thea, 'send them to the outer islands, don't put any ship in the air in case they shoot them down.' Temple guards plus Esmeralda and Kqean's teams rushed to obey, Ali and the team looked for danger coming on to them.

'We never had control, did we?' Kqean asked Marcus.

'You might be fighting for justice but am fighting for tomorrow,' Marcus spoke to them all but his eyes came to rest on Wilvanra.

'What has changed that you must fight now?' Thea asked.

'Everything,' he whispered.

The two halves of the Descendant clashed in order to take full control but someone already held that position. *Was this person really just letting them fight it out?* Ali thought. 'The orb,' she spoke out.

'What is in the orb?' asked Thea.

'I don't know but I think Alexander does,' growled Marcus, scanning the crowd.

Suddenly, the very sea in front of them began to boil. 'He is here!' shouted Philip.

'Get everyone back!' yelled Thea. People who had been scrambling to get on boats were now being pulled off them and running from the water. 'Open the doors of the Volt and Library,' ordered Thea. 'No one enters but Atlanteans and the buildings must not take any hits.'

Yuki picked up Rex and gave him to her mother. 'I love you all but hurry,' said Yuki, pushing her family towards the Volt doors.

'Battle stations!' shouted Marcus, Artemis and hundreds of crew from the Erbus and Veracity rushed around the temple, guns and magic ready.

Dark shapes began to appear just under the surface of the water. The wind picked up, jostling Ali's hair until she could feel magic and motions mixing.

'Spilt the crowd!' shouted Philip as they ran down the steps but there were too many people running everywhere.

'I can't find a line,' shouted Ali.

'I give them a line' said Philip, using his green magic, he marked out the middle of the square, people noticed the magic and stepped away.

'Into the Library or Volt! Now!' cried Thea. Direction combined with a bright green instruction, the crowd syphoned into the Volt and Library, depending on their side of the expanding line. 'Ali, keep them here and protect their backs.'

Ali stood on the green line and raised great two shields over the spilt crowds as they poured into the Volt and Library. Covering two large areas was difficult and Ali tried to concentrate on the people and not the enemy crawling out of the water, small submarines and soldiers in marine suits. The steps of the Volt and Library were still covered in people. Ali was not sure how many hits the force field could take 'We need more time,' Ali pleaded, the sight of soldiers wading out the sea striking fear not only in her but in the crowd too.

'A hot and cold weather on the front should slow them down,' said Philip.

Yuki froze, the water in front of them catching soldiers in the ice and Jenks lit fire to the steps. 'It won't hold them for long,' Yuki cried.

The soldiers removed their helmets, revealing faces as Ali recognised the Lucast triplets, Shamor, Ralfa, and Marwex. Ali scanned the water. Where were Darshan and Kye? And more importantly, Alexander.

'We are ready for them,' said Marcus, joining them at the bottom of the temple steps. The ice cracked and more soldiers emerged from the water. Someone took control of the fire from Jenks and extinguished it.

As the enemy took their first steps on Atlantis, they ran to meet them. The fire was thrown by both sides and magic blasts of purples, greens, blues, reds and yellows filled the air above and the space between the rushing armies.

Ali collected as much magic as she could while Yuki blasted soldiers with ice, sending them flying back into the water. Jenks was taking out the fire and throwing in his own. Philip was targeting people with guns who could hit the Volt or Library and hurt the people inside. Wilvanra was using her light magic, raining sparks that momentarily blinded soldiers as they moved closer. She stopped, not wanting to blind the wrong side. The armies clashed and battle cries rang out. Hand to hand fighting began, Ali, making sure she only had the enemy in front of her, released the power in a multi-coloured energy wave. The wave punched a hole right through the enemy line, clear to the water where the soldiers landed. But there was something in the water, a shape much larger than soldiers and submersibles.

AHH! A mechanical roar deafened everyone and suddenly chains emerged from the water whipping through the air.

'Erbus and Veracity Fire!' shouted Marcus into a radio. Ali turned to see the guns of the great ships revolving to face the monster, but as they did, some of the submersibles began to rise from the water, an air front had opened and they weren't ready.

'By the gods, fire on all ships!' roared Marcus, 'and get ours in the air now.'

The newly born airships began to fire and some veered to the sides of the battlefield, flying alongside in front of the Volt and Library. Ali didn't know if they were trying to get behind them or attack the people. She couldn't let either happen and she grabbed the ships and threw them back toward the sea.

'Ali!' Reece shouted but it was too late. She had taken her eyes from the battle in front of her and she suddenly felt a cold chain wrap itself around her waist.

'Ahhh!' she screamed as she was yanked into the air high above the square. Ali didn't know if she going to pass out or be sick. Ships were flying by her and firing. Other people were captured by the chains and were being flung around the place, too. One of the men was then dropped over the sea and another man was plunged into death. Ali didn't have any air to fight and just reacted by throwing a bubble around her head as she was dragged into the water.

There was a war under the water, among the ruins Merfolk battle Descendant in submersibles. The water boiled, where magic was released and in the middle of the chaos, the mechanical sea monster played conductor over the battle. The bulbous body of the beast was supported by many thick steel tentacles rotating and the many chains moving, keeping all maybe attackers at bay. Ali was too scared to scream, she tried to break of the chain. She had to get to the surface, she had no power beneath the waves.

The chain began to tighten around her, black spots appeared flickered on the edge of her vision. Ali could lose her air bubble and drown, that was if the beast did not crush her first. She was being pulled deeper into the water finally the chain held her in front of the golden eyes of the beast.

Ali struggled against the chain but it was no use and she began to lose the oxygen in her bubble. Suddenly, the chain connecting her to the beast broke as it was hit by a blue blast of magic. Ali, still wrapped in the chain, fell to the seafloor. Esmeralda appeared before her and placed a hand on her bubble and Ali could feel the oxygen level rise. Ali pulled the chain from around and looked to the surface and she could see chains and the enemy drivers looking for her. Esmeralda grabbed her arm and she swam through the streets of the drowned Atlantis. They swam inside a low building, Ali guessed it was a shop once upon by the large stone space where there were widows.

'We can't go into the new city, too many people are there and I don't want the beast hanging over my people but we might be able to lose them here in the old quarter.' Esmeralda spoke of her planned.

Ali nodded her agreement.

'Do you have any power down here?' Esmeralda asked.

'No, the air, I can't touch it, I can keep this in place, but I think that is it,' Ali said pointing her bubble.

'Alright, too many to fight and we are too slow to swim through a gap, so our next best option is to create a distraction or try and make it to the temple although, Marcus may have blocked that entrance by now to stop Alexander coming up behind them on the island.'

'So the best option is a distraction?' choked Ali in disbelief, waving her flowing hair out of her face. 'I am no good down here to you.'

'Yes, we need you back up there, but wait, that's it! I will bring the sky down here to you,' Esmeralda beamed.

'What? How is that possible?' Ali asked wonder.

'We will have to be fast because they will see it right away.'

'See what?'

'An entrance to the sky is a whirlpool of Merfolk.'

'A whirlpool sounds more like a distraction, I am not sure I want to be inside one.'

'I won't be able to hold it for long, but it should give you time to get to the real surface,' said Esmeralda, sneaking a glance of outside. 'They are coming. We don't have time, it's now, or never.' She hissed.

'Okay, but never doesn't sound too bad,' said Ali, shaking her head. Her hair followed the movement.

Esmeralda smiled, 'It takes time to create one, so I can't bring the whirlpool right on top of us or they will find us too soon,' and glanced again for danger. 'I will create one out there and we must swim to it.'

Ali nodded, a plan, any kind of plan, even as crazy as this one, was reassuring her. Esmeralda sat low in the coral-encrusted window and Ali sat opposite her, looking for danger, which was getting closer. Driving soldiers swung torches and the great beast began to move delicately through the ruins while still battling Merfolk, which were now attacking it.

Esmeralda frowned in concentration. 'Someone has got in for you up there.'

'Yes, that would the very man at the head of the army himself,' said Ali, pressing herself into stone to keep low.

Then the surface water began to spin and a watery cone started to twist down to the seafloor a short distance from them.

The whirlpool caught the attention of the soldiers and the beast and they began to move toward it. 'We need to move now! They will be careful not to get caught up in the current but we need to move ahead of them.' They emerged from the shop, swam low, keeping to the ruins. Esmeralda had her hand outstretched to the whirlpool, drawing it deeper, the other keeping Ali's hand, Ali could feel the pull of current strong now. They stopped the whirlpool now on the seabed in a space void of ruins and surrounded by fallen columns. Maybe it was once an old square.

They heard and felt a rumbling sound vibrate through the water and suddenly a dark shadow passed over them. They look up to see a column fly overhead, passing through the whirlpool. 'I think the sea monster is on to us! You must hurry,' said Esmeralda, letting go of her arm.

'Nooo!' shouted Ali but she was swept away by the current and pulled into the whirlpool and pushed through the swirling wall of water, hitting the stone steps hard. Her clothes were heavy with water and stuck to her skin, restricting her movements. She wipes her hair that had become plastered to face away from her eyes. Coughing, Ali felt she could breathe fully and felt her power-slowing coming back to her as she lay under the sky. The cone of water suddenly began to narrow. Esmeralda! Ali shouted as the cone closed. Ali was dragged spinning upwards and outwards. Dizzy, Ali could barely tell she was at a level with the sea now, she vomited and inhale see water. Wading and coughing, Ali turned herself in the direction of shore and slowly swam to the steps.

She crawled over broken stone and glass, hiding behind a large rock she tucked in her knees to make herself a smaller target. Ali peeked behind the rock but the whirlpool had collapsed, Ali moved back against the rock.

Bang! Ali looked up to see the surface battle, which still raged on. She was in no-man's-lands. Not a good placc to be but behind enemy lines was worse. Ali risked another look back at the sea. Esmeralda!

The sea monster breached the surface while throwing columns and ruin rubble at the island. Ali knew she needed to stand and fight again. Ali blocked as many as she could but the stone weighted tons, she could risk dropping the stone back into the water in case it hit their people. Ali let them fall onto the flat just above the steps. She could see other Sylphs doing the same. Ali was beginning to shake, tiring she needed to retreat back or she would become an easy target for the enemy. She slowly moved backward but tripped over the broken ground. Someone grabbed her arm and pulled her up. Ali wanted to scream thinking it was the wrong side but looking up she could see Jenks covered in sweat and blood.

'Come on, Ali, we are almost back,' he panted.

They hastily made their way back and to Yuki's side. 'Ali, thank the gods you're back, I thought you were dead when the creature got you!' Yuki exclaimed.

'I had help, this is the second time that Esmeralda has saved my life,' Ali puffed.

'Did you see Alexander down there?' Jenks asked.

'No, just lots more of them.'

They had been fighting for hours, exhausted they dropped behind rumble for shelter. The other side must have been feeling it too, as the fire lost its intensity and frequency. Their food unsurprised was battered but Ali didn't care someone had created a supply line for the food to the field and she was extremely grateful. Yuki's water bottle had taken a hit along the way Ali shared hers.

'So how everyone's love lives?' wondered Reece.

'What? I don't think the middle of the battle is a place to talk about our love lives,' choked Jenks.

'I got enough love in my life, I got my family and friends, I don't need another relationship that everyone thinks is more important than my relationships that I hold with them.' declared Yuki.

'I agree there is no such thing as true love. It's all just love,' Ali chipped in. Yuki and Ali had extensive talks on the subject. They had been through cheating and breakups and in the end, being with themselves made them happier.

'You're alone in the classic romance there,' laughed Jenks.

'Ah, I was just hoping for one of us, people won't even talk to me anymore. I think it's because of who we are now,' groaned Reece.

'And who are we?' asked Ali.

'I am not sure anymore,' he shrugged.

'If you do the right thing, the right people will come along,' smiled Jenks.

They ate in silence until they could hear someone grumbling closer, Captain Philip crawling on his stomach, dragging himself over to their hiding place. 'We got reports of the next wave of attack coming in. They say Alexander will be leading the charge,' Captain Philip huffed.

'How do we know,' asked Reece?

'Report from the water. The beast is on the move, that's where the commands for their army have been coming from so it must be where Alexander is. The strongest vessel in the water.' Philip said, making himself more comfortable on the ground.

'Where did the information come from?' gulped Ali, worrying about Esmeralda. 'How is the battle below going?'

'I don't know, I got it from another Captain, he only said the message has to go on. As for the rest of battle, it has taken a lull like here, but I think they have taken more losses if Alexander is on the move.'

They were all silent for a while, things were going to get harder. Ali felt sick thinking about what was going to happen, all her team was with her and that was comforting but at the same time, they were all in danger with all of Atlantis. Ali jolted upright, 'It's happening again, is this history repeating it's self this is the second battle to be fought here.'

Chapter 24

The Last King

'An oracle told that history would repeat itself he said, Time is running out. The clock is going back, the battle happened here once before and it is here again,' explained Ali.

'We won the last time,' Jenks insisted hopefully.

'We are outnumbered this time,' Captain Philip stated flatly.

'And there's the orb. Did we have that the last time?' wondered Reece.

'I don't know, maybe. We had and didn't use or it was created after,' Ali speculated.

'Samdar must have found something out about the orb when it was taken,' Yuki questioned. 'Maybe he is awake?'

Ali looked over to the Volt, it would not be hard to get over, there it was, still on their side just. The enemy had taken half the square but they still controlled the higher ground; the steps leading to Volt and the Library, plus the temple at their backs. They could not lose this ground or the people inside could be at risk.

'We should talk to Thea and Marcus first and see what they are planning about the new report,' asserted Captain Philip.

Thea and Marcus had moved to the back of the battlefield at the temple steps. They slowly crawled in the open and walked half hunched between boulders back to the temple. No shots had been fired in a while but the temple guards were on high alert. Maybe there was a chance of sleeping tonight. The temple guards let them pass and they walked up the side steps out of sight to the main square in shadows now.

Thea, Wilvanra, Marcus, Kqean, Artemis and the Line were gathered around a table where maps of surface and lower Atlantis were being held down with stones.

'You have to hear the news then,' said Thea, looking up from the maps.

172

'No,' confessed Philip.

'I am sorry to tell you this but Samdar passed away before night fell.'

'But his injuries were not serious!' uttered Ali, shocked.

'Yes, but infirmary was under stress before the attack and now it is barely coping,' expressed Thea. 'We need to cut this battle short, a slow the fighting has helped us recover somewhat but we can't go on fighting through the night or we may not see tomorrow.'

'Maybe Alexander coming to us is not a bad idea,' ventured Artemis. 'It would shorten the battle one way or another.'

Ali thought, *he was trying to find hope in war*. Ali stopped hearing the battle talk and she thought the rest of the team did too, they had lost a pillar of Atlantis in Samdar.

'Why don't you and your team get some sleep while you can? The other teams are taking shifts,' suggested Thea. 'I will let you know if anything changes, Alexander is taking his time out there for now, by the latest reports.'

They found some empty cots in an alcove outside Thea's office. 'I am going to talk with Artemis's team to see what schedule they have made up for the night,' said Philip, leaving them there.

They were too tired to need Babylon Lanterns and only took their boots off. Ali dreamed of a shining orb and swirls of colours surrounding her, she reached to touch one but she was suddenly sucked inside of the orb. Inside there was no up or down, just moving colours and Ali couldn't find a way out.

Ali snapped awake just before someone banged on their door. 'The second wave is there,' he shouted. It sounded like one of Marcus men. Outside in the main temple, teams gathered around there and listened to orders. Philip never came back and Ali began to worry, maybe he would be with Thea. After all, they were meant to be in her team and she was meant to separate as the High Guard but thankfully no one had mentioned that yet.

'You lot get over here,' shouted Philip.

Ali was relieved to hear him but he sounded angry and when they finally pushed through the crowd, he looked vexed too. 'Right, we are sticking with Thea as Plan B, at the temple, the other teams are spreading out across the square.'

'What was Plan A?' asked Jenks.

'We are not Plan A, so we can't know about it,' sighed Philip.

173

Thea and the Line stood on the temple steps, it felt strange to stand back and watch as other teams took positions in the square in the dark before and not to be with them.

A sobering silence settled over the square and Ali could almost hear the waves gently lapping down at the docks. Ali felt the wait slaying it seem to stretch to eternity, then the sound of metal scraping against stone filled the air. It was coming from the water but Ali couldn't see anything.

'It's here' Yuki whispered.

'Light the fires,' ordered Thea. Fires jumped to life along with the steps of the Volt and the Library. But the docks and whatever was coming ashore still lay in darkness.

'Jenks will you please give us a little more light,' asked Philip.

'Yes, captain,' Jenks released a yellow sphere from his hands and threw it towards the sea. Just over the shore, it exploded and showered the dock in light. The great sea beast, using its many tentacles, was crawling onshore. Its golden eyes came to life at being uncovered. It let out a thunderous roar.

Footsteps from behind them made her start with fright. Marcus, Artemis and Kqean walked out of the temple in full battle dress.

'Our blessings are with you all,' said Thea.

Marcus nodded and they made their way down the steps and into the square. There, Kqean raised a white flag and held it high for all to see before the beast in the emerging light.

'Please tell me that's not Plan A?' asked Reece.

'I, Marcus Shadow, challenge you Alexander Shadow for the position of master descendant,' shouted Marcus.

The beast roared again, moving one of its arms to the side revealing a hidden door. The door opened and out stepped Kye, Darshan, and Alexander. They walk to the centre of the square, standing opposite Marcus, his second, and the councillor.

'I accepted your challenge for the seat of the king,' said Alexander.

'That's Plan A, a duel in the middle of the city,' coughed Reece.

'Shouldn't I be down there?' asked Ali

'You can't duel now because you are a High Guard plus the fact of under-tested powers, you're not in control yet,' said Wilvanra. 'But this is hope, remember they are more battle wore than we are.'

'But what about the orb?' asked Yuki.

174

'We don't know but until then it is a fair duel,' said Thea. 'Arcwqil will oversee it from down there too.'

Marcus was the first to strike, casting red lightning down on Alexander. Darshan threw up a dome shield protecting them but Ali could hear the lightning cracking as it rained down on the shield.

Alexander wasn't laughing, this duel was not a game. *Marcus was his match,* Ali thought. Alexander roll one fireball and then split it into many balls as it drew closer to its target.

Kqean created a water snake, which snapped and caught the balls with its twisting body, putting out the ground fires.

Marcus created a lightning vortex and sent it spinning over Alexander, raining down strikes. Darshan cast another shield but Ali could see his knees shaking from a distance.

Alexander threw fire down on the ground and from the flames he called a tiger of an unnaturally large size, its claws scorched the stone, its eyes like black coals.

Kqean called upon the water snake again, arching him to meet the tiger in the eyes. The snake bared its fangs and water dripped from its open jaw.

The snake lunged, wrapping itself around the neck of the tiger. Steam rose from the fight as they rolled across the ground.

The tiger released itself from the snake and lunged at Marcus, who stood so still Ali thought, *he must have his eyes closed, not to move but to see that coming at you.*

Artemis threw a wall of stone between them and the fire beast. The tiger tore at the wall but then backed off as the wall began to take shape. The stone transformed into a winged lion leapt at the tiger. Both crashed to the ground, the tiger disappeared as the fire without and the lion melted into the ground.

Another round, thought Ali anxiously, looking at Yuki who looked hopeful 'They are doing well' Yuki nodded.

Marcus created a web of lightning over Alexander, he sent the web spinning. Kye and Darshan looked up, worried. Threads of the lightning web snapped out at different times and places test for weakness in the shield. Kye stepped from the shield and jumped through the red web and threw fire at Marcus, who just dodged in time but let his web flicker out. Alexander won't survive another round, Kye couldn't match lightning and Darshan was weakening like his shields.

Alexander threw back his head to the sky 'Aaah' he shouted. Flame gathered in the sky, morphing into a dragon. Kqean and Artemis called on their creatures. They didn't wait for the dragon to make the first move. Alexander must have been expecting this because the dragon faded as the snake and lion attacked. Alexander threw fire straight at Marcus.

A ball of fire ripped through the simple shield and struck Marcus in the chest. He stumbled but did not fall. The amour saved him but the blow still must have hurt.

Marcus was now down on one knee and Alexander was next in line for the throne. Alexander threw a dragger. 'There will be no more of you' and lit the blade of the knife on fire.

'No!' Marcus struggled to his feet, 'I am not done yet.'

Alexander looked worried, thought Ali, *he must not be able to go another round either, he couldn't keep the dragon in the sky.*

'You have fallen,' Alexander hissed.

'You will have to do better than that,' growled Marcus.

'No, it is my time to rise! Arcwqil, the orb belongs to me now,' called Alexander.

Time seemed to stop and the only person who could move was the Master Descendant as he walked down the steps through the fire, holding an orb of blue and silver. An orb that Ali had held before.

'Arcwqil?' cried Thea, 'No, Noooo!'

'This is for Atlantis, we need a new king,' said Arcwqil, handing for the orb to Alexander.

'Attack,' shouted Thea. 'Philip, get the orb now!'

They ran down to the square but the fighting between Atlantis and the Descendants had erupted again, slowing them down. Arcwqil and the Line turned on Marcus, Artemis and Kqean. While Alexander made is his way to the centre of the square protected by Darshan and Kye. He placed the orb on the ground and Atlantis shook for the third time. They were too late. The orb began to float and shine.

'The ancient power is mine. I am the king,' Alexander laughed, reaching out the claim the power.

'Ahh!' Alexander roared in pain, snatching his hand back burn and smoking hand. The ground beneath began to crack and shift, the last of Atlantis was sinking.

'This is what you wanted, Arcwqil,' shouted Thea. 'There will be nothing left of Atlantis now. You will cast last ruins into the deep.'

'The orb's energy is what is breaking up the city, we can't let it sink any further, we need to stop it now!' urged Philip, ducking and blasting green magic at descendants.

'Did you not see what it just did to Alexander's hand?' Reece screeched, turning to take a purple energy blast to the shoulder, 'and I don't think gloves are going to save ya,' he yelled, firing his gun back in the magic direction.

'Ali, can you move it?' asked Philip.

Ali cast her powers over it and tried to pull it away from the centre. 'No, I can't, like someone else is pulling on it, keeping it there,' Ali puffed. She looked to Arcwqil the master was in their mists the whole time. 'Samdar! I think Arcwqil went to Samdar. Samdar knew something about the orbs.'

'What if it is not someone but it's twin? Remember, the orbs only react when they are in the presence of their other twin,' Yuki yelled, shooting an ice blast. 'Maybe this is why the orb left Atlantis. They tried to hide it.'

'The other twin must be buried. If they are locked to each, how do we undo them?' asked Jenks.

'Their energy if I could take that, then they could be separated,' Ali wondered.

'No, Ali,' Philip turned on her. 'You can't. It is one thing gaining that which is being thrown around freely, channelling it and redirecting is still untested power Ali. It is different to get involved in a reaction. That is even if you could, but let's not risk this, there has to be another way.'

'None of you are worthy,' roared Arcwqil, leaving the Line to finish off Marcus and his team. Arcwqil rushed towards the orb.

Ali knew they needed to take back control or lose the rest of the city and everyone still standing, hiding in the Volt and the Library and those falling right now. Suddenly, she felt alone. She missed her family more than. Anything, she never sends that postcard. Petrified, but let her guard down and reached for the energy surging between the orbs. History was repeating itself. The city was drowning again.

The orb let out a pulse of energy, it send Arcwqil flying who was the closest to it and the whole battlefield was flattened. The city stopped shaking and Philip rolled back to Ali, 'Nooo!'

Ali wanted to let go of the energy was she trapped into. It was no longer running through the orbs but through her. The energy that was shaking the city could destroy her now. Her vision began to flicker, but not to darkness, but to another place and Ali realised another time. Ali could stay here longer because she had been here before.

*

Yuki pulled Reece up. The pulse had knocked everyone down, all except Ali. Who had moved closer and now was standing right before the orb.

'She stopped it,' gasped Reece. Looking around the square was silence and a light breeze lifted the ash from the ground.

'I don't think it is over,' worried Yuki, fear sparking down her spine, grabbing Reece. They ran, jumping and dodging fallen soldiers.

Thea, Philip and Jenks rushed to Ali but they see could Yuki and Reece bounce off a shield.

'Ali' Yuki screamed, clawing at the shield.

'Ali, it's your captain. You did it, the city is safe but you need to let go now,' Philip urged.

'Ali Redfish, stand down,' ordered Thea.

'I don't think she can hear us,' Jenks summarised looking into Ali's face through the shield.

Esmeralda pushed through an army, no longer fighting but struggling to its feet. 'What is happening?' Esmeralda shouted, running towards Thea. 'There was a massive magic pulse through the water—' Esmeralda stopped short. 'By the Drowned King.'

'Indeed, something not seen since the kings I fear,' Thea whispered.

Arcwqil pushed himself up from the ground and the Line gathered around him, ready for orders. They were so close now to the power that he could taste it. The ancient power was close. 'Alexander,' he growled. 'Get up and take Marcus out, if we can't have the power, they can't have it.'

'Ali's powers are new to her but they are of older days' The Line whispered.

'Yes, yes, the fable of the Descendants says that in the last days of ruin the king's power would rise but her connection will matter little, when we hold the orb the power will pass to us the real power,' Arcwqil assured.

Alexander had retreated from the centre, his hand still in agony and by the gods, the smell of it. He wanted to strangle Arcwqil with his good hand for what he had done to him.

The Line whispered, 'He is not worthy. The orb burned him. He is no son of Hades.'

'Of course, he is not the one now, but we must take out Marcus first then we will take king's power,' he hissed.

'The High Guard,' they whispered back.

Arcwqil looked to Ali but he could see in her eyes she wasn't here anymore, she was seeing something different. 'She must be from the line of kings. It's why the city shook when she walked through the arch. It was a connection to the old. Power, we will kill her too.'

The Line stood as one, long cloaks sweeping up dust; they drew power.

Marcus looked at Wilvanra. She shouldn't be here but it was her fight too. They weren't just fighting for each other anymore. Marcus moved his focus on Alexander, his magic spend and they were both injured. This was more than a fair fight Marcus marshalled.

Wilvanra could feel the energy shift, there was power back in play not just radiating from Ali. Wilvanra turned, six men and women strode across the square magic in hand.

Kye didn't know who he was fighting for. Alexander had been denied the power, so who held the power over him?

*

The army rushed at Ali and the mysterious women. Ali threw up a shield to protect them. 'Who are you?' asked Ali through gritted teeth, trying to hold the shield up as warriors threw magic and metal at it.

'To others, I am not who, but what,' she smiled sadly.

'What are you to others?' asked Ali

'A curse.'

Ali felt her shield slip. 'What are you to them?' she cried.

'The power at Atlantis.'

The shield broke and before Ali could step closer to the woman, a priest pushed an orb into Ali's hands.

'Finish it, my king.'

Ali looked at the women, confused.

'It has already happened, Ali.'

*

Ali blinked but the orb was no longer in her hands but before her, just like the Atlantis of the present. She was the ancient power of Atlantis and the curse, no, not just the power. She was the power at Atlantis, she was still here. The orb's power still pulsed painfully through her. This is the moment repeating itself: this was history paused. The last king was killed before he could take full control before he drown the last piece of the city.

The fighting raged. *To help them or take away, what they were fighting over?* Ali thought. Ali could see that Alexander and Arcwqil had joined forces fighting side by side. Kye kept their side back with fire. Kqean and Esmeralda moved up to battle the fire directly and Yuki stepped around the shield and shot ice daggers that hit Kye, one finding its target in his leg and the fire fell with him, their side advancing now. Another blow from their side and Ali needed to know she knew what was needed to be done but she looked around the battlefield again.

Wilvanra and Marcus fought alongside as much as they fought for each other and their future, both had done wrong but were trying to make it right. Arcwqil and Thea, their elders, were fighting for the past but maybe we just needed to learn from it and not live it. Finally, she looked at her friends they were just fighting for right now.

Ali took the blue and silver floating orb from the air. It was the cursed orb Ali could feel and see in her mind, magic being ripped from humans. However, this orb was something more, a key, the ruins on her hand came to burn. A key that could only be turned by a descendant not of Hades but of a king, a human, who wanted the power of the gods. Blood magic.

Did she want to keep that power, power was convenient, power was addictive, but was it who she is? Who she wanted to be? Ali thought, the power of Atlantis had caused so much pain and was still causing pain and it was killing her now.

Ali couldn't let go of the energy so let her senses expand. There! Ali could feel another energy burning like a star. The orb's twin. Reaching for the ground, Ali called upon the other orb, it was deep. Ali rose into the air calling higher and higher. The ground below her broke and emerged a silver shining orb floating up to her. As the orb float upwards, Atlantis rose from the sea. Waves retreated from the old city streets. Temples once submerged for aeons sounded with the wind whistling through their columns. Boats and ships became landlocked and the people stopped fighting.

The Merfolk city could be seen clearly below the water from the old docks, where the waves began to lap once more. Some islands joined once more to the mainland while former islands rose too, from the sea. Ali took the orb into her other hand and rose high above Atlantis, here she brought the orbs together. The key orb flashed and broke into dust. The second orb expanded and burst into light, Ali swore she saw a woman's shape in that light. Ali watched as she disappeared, becoming the wind and clouds.

The twin orbs were a key and a chest, Ali thought, the chest holding the power of Atlantis and the key a vessel to channel it. The king wanted more power and tried to channel human magic but created the cursed orb. Ali was not quite ready to touch down. Where would she stand? Where would they stand with humans? Looking to the island of death it was still an island, which made sense, Ali thought of all the people who had given the lives. Lowering herself, the temple hid the island from view but Ali knew that justice would be granted to all those living and dead. Ali also felt they were strong enough for a new world.

Finally touching Atlantis again, Ali could see everyone had laid down the weapons. The Line had lost the power of the first kings and the curse of the last king that would have helped them was broken. Ali wasn't sure who she saw: a goddess, pure magic, a human, someone like her, but she was free and Ali suddenly felt free too.

Ali's team rushed to hug her with Philip and Thea following. 'So you were missing piece a link to the ancient power,' said Thea raising an eyebrow

'That power is long gone now.' She looked down at her hands. The ancient runes still remained but now faded, Ali felt relief and looking up at the sky, she smiled.

'I believe you,' Thea smiled.

'What happens now?' Ali asked Thea.

'While I was enjoying retirement before the kidnapping retreat, I think I will stick around for a bit.' Thea nodded and walked back to the battlefield now a political theatre.

The world would see them now, they had lost that ancient power long ago when the last king wanted everything, but he couldn't control that power. When he tried to channel more the key became a curse. But they got their city back and that had to mean something right. Ali smiled at her team.